I0788128

Petr Nemirovskiy

SCREAM OF THE FALCON

M•Graphics Publishing

Boston • 2024 • Chicago

Petr Nemirovskiy
Scream of the Falcon. *A novel*

Edited by David Yerganian

Copyright © 2024 by Petr Nemirovskiy

ISBN 978-1-960533-44-9 (Hardcover)
ISBN 978-1-960533-45-6 (Paperback)
ISBN 978-1-960533-46-3 (Ebook)

Library of Congress Control Number: 2024940658

Published by M•Graphics | Boston, MA
　　www.mgraphics-books.com
　　mgraphics.books@gmail.com

Cover Design by Larisa Studinskaya

Book Design by Bagriy & Company | Chicago, IL
　　www.bagriycompany.com
　　printbookru@gmail.com

Printed in the United States of America

Contents

PART FOUR

PART FIVE

PART SIX

PART ONE

Hooked

Taking my fishing pole and a bag, I walked out of the one-bedroom co-op in Marine Park, Brooklyn, that I had recently bought and headed toward the salt marsh. It was early morning. A white dove which had nested nearby a few months ago suddenly descended to the ground. Standing motionless, it stared at me, cooing. "What's up, buddy?" I asked. After apologizing for not having any bread or crackers, the dove took off, and I continued on my way.

Standing on some huge rocks by the shore of the marsh, I baited my hook and cast my line out into the bay, then played the waiting game. It was quiet, a light breeze chasing small waves.

Not far from me stood a man, roughly in his fifties, of medium height and decent build. He had a pleasant appearance, not without charm. Short wavy hair, combed back, framed his oval face. Upon closer scrutiny, his clear, penetrating eyes drew attention, and a good-natured smile played on his lips. He was also fishing. Squinting, he looked out somewhere into the distance, where boats chugged into the bay and the outline of the bridge was faintly visible. At times, he seemed to be deep in thought. I'd seen this man here a few times. We'd engage in fishing-related banter, like the best way to catch bluefish and such. So far in our short conversations, we hadn't asked for personal particulars—like each other's name, occupation, or residence. Since he was carrying only minimal fishing gear, I concluded that he also lived nearby, and, like me, was not an avid fisherman, but came here to breathe in the fresh, salty ocean air, spend some time alone, and basically relax amid the surroundings.

I watched as he would repeatedly cut off a large piece of baitfish with a knife, put it on a hook, and—with a precise motion—cast his line. During one of his casts, a greedy seagull gliding by suddenly swooped on the flying bait, snapped it up, and tried to fly away with it! The man pulled on the rod to snatch it back, and after a short, somewhat comical struggle between the two unusual combatants, the bird finally surrendered, let go of the fish, and took off with angry cries. It flew to where the water was "boiling"—a school of bluefish was in a feeding frenzy on smaller fish. What the bluefish didn't get below, voracious seagulls attacked from above as the smaller fish tried to escape.

"Such beauty," said the man, putting his hand over his face to shield the sun. "Bluefish in the salt marsh are very active now, in late summer, early fall."

"Yes, and it's a pretty amazing sight," I agreed, squatting on a rock.

"Whoa!" he shrieked, pulling on his rod to reel in a catch.

"Probably a bluefish," I guessed.

"Let's hope it's a good bluefish!" He replied.

It was. He soon had it landed and began pulling the hook from its mouth.

"Come on, baby, open your mouth!" he pleaded with the fish. With one swift motion, one blow to the head with a rock, the fish was dead. He calmly took his folding knife out and began to clean it. He removed the scales with extraordinary precision, especially around the fins and gills. Then he sliced open the fish's belly and just as carefully began to remove the intestines.

I observed him, focused on his task with a bloodied knife in his hand, then looked at the gutted and meticulously cleaned fish.

"Looks like you're performing fish surgery," I commented.

"You're right. I removed its gallbladder and transplanted the liver."

"Are you a doctor?"

"Yes, I'm a surgeon. I'm also head of the Emergency Room at Bethlehem Hospital. What's your name?"

"Ben. And yours?"

"Michael. Michael Harris. It's easy to remember."

"Nice to meet you, Dr. Harris."

"You can just call me Michael. Call me whatever you like." We finally got to talking.

"Do you live near here?" I asked.

"Yes, on Fillmore Street."

"So, then, we're neighbors. I live on Gerritsen Avenue."

"What do you do for a living, Ben?"

"I work in a small outpatient clinic with mental health and substance abuse patients."

"So, it seems we're colleagues to some extent. Are you a psychiatrist?"

"Almost, I'm a psychotherapist."

"Do you like your job?"

"In general, yes. I like to work with patients. But the salary is low and the benefits are lousy there."

"Understood. Are you married?"

"Divorced, thank God. Whoa!"

The rod in my hands suddenly bent violently. I pulled it toward me and immediately sensed a strong fish was hooked.

"Wow! This looks serious, no joke," exclaimed Dr. Harris, staring at my bent rod.

I spun the reel handle as the fish veered either far left or far right. Only a large fish could have grabbed the big hook I'd attached to the line. When the fish would swim toward me, the line weakened, as if it had fallen off. I only had to spin the reel a few times and the line became taut again. Then the rod bent sharply, and the fish, after some rest, continued the fight.

"Ah!!!" I yelled, getting exhausted from the tension.

Sweat suddenly streamed down my face like rain. I had no idea that pressure could make it flow like a flash flood. My T-shirt and even underwear—everything—became wet with sweat. I kept spinning the reel, doubting that I could bring the fish in.

"It's a shark!" yelled Dr. Harris as I dragged a huge sand shark onto the rocks, breathing heavily.

It flopped around with an open jaw, scarlet blood spilling over its slippery gray body and flat white stomach from where the hook had punctured it. I pressed the shark's face firmly against the rock. I wanted to kill it, that's how much I hated it at that moment. At the same time, I wanted to kiss its bloodied mouth—that's how much I loved it.

Sweat was still rolling down my face. The shark was thrashing its tail, trying to get out of my grasp.

"Let me help you." Dr. Harris came over and held the shark down as I tried to pull the hook out of its bloody jaws.

I finally succeeded, and squeezing the shark tightly by the gills, threw it back into the water. The shark immediately disappeared beneath the surface.

"Swim baby, you're free."

"Good job, Ben," said Dr. Harris. He was staring at me, as if judging my capabilities. "Listen, man, would you like to work in our hospital? I'd love to have you in our Emergency Room."

"What kind of work would it be?"

"In a nutshell, we have a special zone in the ER where we place drug addicts and alcoholics, as well as suicidal and homicidal—in short, all the 'cuckoos.' I desperately need a specialist with experience working with these types of folks. As you can imagine it's never boring. I think you'd enjoy it. And the hospital has great benefits—insurance, an annual raise, plenty of vacation time. Think about it. Take my number and call me when you make a decision."

"I'm giving you the answer right now. Yes."

"Yellow Gowns"

It had been a few months since I'd started working in the ER. It was a decent-sized private hospital in downtown Brooklyn. I worked the day shift, but if needed I would stay late. I commuted there by car—about a forty-minute drive.

As Dr. Harris said, inside the ER was a special section dedicated to "cuckoos." Some of them came into the ER on their own, others came by ambulance, and the rest were brought in by the police. Some had their hands cuffed and their feet shackled. Some were so drunk they couldn't stand. There was a non-stop drop-off of overdosed drug addicts. Suicidal patients were also often brought in. At times, fights broke out between patients, or they attacked the personnel.

All patients in this section of the ER were dressed in yellow hospital gowns. They had no idea that a yellow gown signaled high alert to staff as opposed to the regular red or blue gowns. Police and security guards always had a presence in this area, and any relocation of a "yellow gown" immediately caught their attention. The yellow gowns in the ER were labeled "numb nuts" in the "dimwit zone." Sometimes in conversation between staff, things like this would slip: "Should we put this patient with the numb nuts?" or "We have the last available bed in the dimwit zone."

Steven, a large Black psych technician, stood by the high pillar in the center of this zone, performing the role of over-seer—monitoring and maintaining order. Looking at him, it always amazed me how nature could have created such a giant. If any of the patients were ever on the verge of los-ing control, Steven approached them, and in an unwavering voice advised them to calm down and lie back down in bed. If the patient still retained a spark of sanity, just looking at giant Steven would make them comply, albeit with resent-ment. Still, for those that chose to defy him, the police were called to take more drastic measures.

From this section, patients went off in different direc-tions: some proceeded to the "cuckoo ward," some to drug detox. Those handcuffed and shackled were escorted out by the police to precincts. There were also those whose condition had improved after spending some time in the ER on medication; they were sent home. My role was that of a so-called coordinator—along with the doctors, I decided where a yellow gown would be sent.

One of the superstitions of all ER employees is never to utter aloud, "Gee, it's pretty quiet." Even if two-thirds of the beds in the ER are empty and made up with clean sheets, and it's so quiet that you can hear a fly buzz, under no circumstances should you say, "Gee, it's pretty quiet." As a newbie, I inadvertently broke this rule, and my colleagues immediately hissed at me: "Why are you saying that?!" This was because, unexpectedly, like a tornado swooping in on a peaceful village and quickly changing it beyond recogni-tion, the same transformation can happen in the dimwit zone: one moment it's calm and almost empty; the next all the beds are taken—the clean white sheets become stained with blood and dirt; the police pacify one "psycho" yellow gown while doctors administer life-saving medicine to another who has overdosed.

* * *

Such was the atmosphere in my new workplace—some of it familiar and some of it new. Yes, I'd worked with patients like yellow gowns before for many years in my career as a psychotherapist. However, the stress in the ER was incomparably higher than in the small outpatient clinic where I had last worked. Initially, I slept poorly, ate haphazardly, and lost weight.

Despite all that, I liked this place more and more each day. When a shift finally ended, I'd drag myself to the office for a cup of coffee, make some final phone calls, and fill out paperwork. I walked along a long, brightly lit corridor of the ER, nodding to doctors, nurses, and police officers walking toward me. I'd often recall how I met Dr. Harris on the shore of the salt marsh, when I caught that fateful shark. The smell of sea salt, sand, and algae suddenly penetrated my nostrils.

All about My Father

After work I sometimes went to see my father. He lived in a rented one-bedroom apartment in a respectable Brooklyn neighborhood — Bay Ridge. Not long ago, he underwent his third heart surgery, almost immediately following a second one, and he needed care.

Until recently, we saw little of each other and spoke rarely on the phone — ever since he divorced my mother, leaving us to go live with another woman when I was 15. At the time I was glad he departed, since the family scandals and my parents' endless warring — the fault of which was my father's quarrelsome, selfish nature and his heavy drinking — would finally come to an end.

I never felt any deep attachment to him. We were very different people — different in temperament, in values, and in our outlook on life. Nevertheless, he was my father, and as a child, I respected his strength and power. To be honest, back then, I was afraid of him and poorly understood him. When he was drunk, there were instances where he beat me. I tried to go unnoticed, even hiding sometimes from him in closets so I wouldn't get in his way and then under his hands. When I was a teenager, I was always in a hurry to finish my homework before he got home from work, and then I'd run to the park, where I played basketball or handball with my friends. I sat there with them late on park benches or on swings at the playground, and we secretly drank beer or smoked weed.

I always hoped I'd receive some sort of kindness and acceptance from my father. Whatever he did, no matter how much he insulted me, I still waited desperately for him to show me love. On rare occasions he did, but only while drunk—when he would hug me. I remember vividly how he'd press his prickly, unshaven cheek into my face. This rush of tenderness was usually accompanied by some drunken babbling about how I bore the name of his father, who once escaped from the Nazi concentration camp at Auschwitz during the war. "You, Ben, were named after him. Always remember that all men in our family were heroes." When he leaned into me, I grimaced from the stench of vodka. I tensed up inside, waiting for him to back off.

When he got together with that other woman and left us, I let out a sigh of relief. After that, we rarely saw each other and communicated very little. Sometimes I completely forgot about his existence, not seeing or hearing from him for years.

Oddly enough, he suddenly developed a warm relationship with my ex-wife, Sarah, when we were still together. He sometimes came to visit us, showing some grandfatherly interest in Veronica, my daughter. When my wife and I divorced, she moved with Veronica to Boston. My father's relationship with them faded.

A few years ago, the woman with whom he lived eventually got very sick, virtually falling apart. Her adult daughter took her to live with her in Philadelphia, and my father stayed in their apartment in Brooklyn.

Meanwhile, I changed jobs, drank—sometimes often and a lot—and buried my mother. Recently, my father had suddenly reappeared in my life, like a Shakespearean ghost appearing on the eve of a fateful event.

* * *

"Hi, can I come in?"

"Yes, please."

In front of me in the door stood a Black woman, around 34, medium height, slender, in gray sweatpants and a black T-shirt. My eye immediately went to her full, high breasts and her deep, dark eyes.

"My name is Amy. How are you doing? You're Ben, Mark's son, right?"

"Yes, ma'am. And you are…?"

"His home health aide. His doctor requested one for him after his last heart surgery, and it was approved. For now, your father is eligible for five home health aide hours daily, five days per week," she said as we entered the living room.

"Hi, Dad. How are you?"

My father was sitting in a chair watching baseball on TV. His legs were raised on a retractable footrest.

"Hi, Ben. Still alive, as you can see." He smiled, grimacing, with his lips shifted to the left.

I never liked that side smile; it looked more like the grin of some predatory animal.

I sat down on the sofa next to Amy, who was looking at something on her cell phone. I don't know, maybe I sat too close to her, but as soon as I sat on the sofa and put my right hand next to my hip, for some reason Amy immediately rose, as if I posed some danger to her.

"Do you want coffee? Tea?" She asked, stepping a few feet away from me.

"No, thank you."

"And you, Mark, can I get you something to eat or drink?"

"No, not yet."

"Okay." She went into the kitchen, ran the tap water, and began to wash dishes. From where I sat, I saw only the back of her short-sleeved black T-shirt.

I wanted to make love to her. Here and now. Let my father sit in the chair and watch his baseball. I'm going to retire to the bedroom with her — the doorknob there has a lock. What a great thing it is that he was given this home aide! She won't mind making love to me, either — it's obvious. These strange, wild thoughts seemed to have arisen on their own, against my will, and swirled through my head like a whirlwind. I rubbed my wrinkled-up forehead with my fingers. Yes, now we're going to retire to the bedroom and make love.

At that moment, Amy looked back, as if she had overheard my inner monologue. She smiled broadly, and her big eyes flashed wildly and eagerly. I looked at and nodded toward the bedroom. She showed me her middle finger with a red-painted fingernail and turned away laughing. I chuckled in response — this meaningful silent dialogue amused me too.

Then I turned to my dad. "How are you, Dad? I think you're better today." I looked at him — this time with the expert gaze of a healthcare professional working in an ER. In my short time in the ER, I had gradually developed a professional clinician's view: this is when you listen to the patient but focus your attention not only on their words but also on whether their face is pale, their breathing rate, in short, any symptoms to determine whether they are critical or not. Now, according to my assessment, though my father was somewhat pale and a bit haggard in appearance after his latest operation, he was still not critical.

"You only think I'm feeling better. In fact, I'm still unwell," he grunted with reproach. "Today, I've had high blood pressure and a headache since this morning." He sighed. "In general, things are bad."

I frowned, feeling sorry for him.

"I called Dr. Shapiro, and he advised me to take a double dose of the blood pressure pills. Let's see how it goes. It's just fucking old age." He reduced the TV volume and lowered the footrest. Then he got up and went to the bathroom.

Former Military Man Dr. Mercy

Each shift in the ER began with morning rounds. The team of doctors and case managers walked through the whole department. The nurses on duty, responsible for certain sections, gave us reports on their patients. After debriefing, we all went to our respective workspaces.

Firstly, I went to the ER administration office. Dr. Harris decided that I was not only a good fisherman but also a very important worker, and I should sit with the administration.

I shared the office with Dr. Adam Mercy, the lead surgeon. He also held the position of co-chair to the ER director. Some time back, before becoming a doctor, Dr. Mercy had served in the army in a special unit, earning the rank of lieutenant colonel. Once during a military operation, something happened to him that he never shared with me, but by his own admission, it changed his life forever. After that incident, he left the army and became a doctor, in his own words, "not to kill anymore, but only to save lives."

Nevertheless, he could talk about his service in the army endlessly. Listening to colorful stories about his various combat operations, sometimes it seemed to me that I was not in an ER in New York talking with a doctor, but at some boot camp in South Carolina, where a heavily armed special unit was readying for deployment to different country on a classified mission.

At first, I thought Dr. Mercy liked to embellish his former military accomplishments, since now at 55 he was slightly overweight, had several medical problems, and barely re-sembled his former military self. He was a real "foodie"—a connoisseur of culinary arts—and was constantly joking around with everyone. In short, he gave the impression of being a kind soul and an epicurean. However, after seeing him handle several critical situations in the course of his job in the ER—which required courage, lightning-speed reac-tions, and the ability to correctly make decisions in the blink of an eye—I concluded that even if Dr. Mercy were embel-lishing his prior feats in the army, it wasn't by that much.

Soul of the Bird

Amy and I met in the park in Union Square. We walked together down the paths, around and around, the mighty crowns of old trees rustling above us. Men turned to stare at us, or rather not us, but at Amy—she was graceful and statuesque. Some time ago in her youth she had taken dance lessons, and clearly it didn't pass unnoticed. However, if judging by strict aesthetic standards, Amy's physique had a minor disproportion: her hips were a bit narrow for such a high, full chest and somewhat broad shoulders.

She wore short jeans that showed her ankles and a bright-red T-shirt, tightly tucked. She colored her hair brown. Thick chunks of mascara covered her eyelashes, and silver specks sparkled on her eyelids. We talked nonstop.

"I come from Georgia; my mother was a teacher, and my father was a mechanic in a car repair shop. I was the youngest child in the family, a little princess," she said. "My mother was a devout woman, took us to church on Sundays, read the Bible to us kids, and taught us to pray. My father died a long time ago from a stroke—he was a crackhead. After that, my mother married another man, and continued to work at a school until her retirement. My dear mommy, she died last year, may her soul rest in peace." Amy rolled her big, dark brown eyes up toward the sky, made the sign of the cross, and put her fingers first to her lips and then to her chest on the left.

"My mother also died recently, two years ago. And my dad used to drink a lot at one point. So, our stories are somewhat similar," I said.

"Yes, you and I are like brother and sister," Amy joked, laughing. She laughed loudly, baring her large, not-quite-straight teeth. Perhaps the crooked teeth were the only flaw of her face, with its soft, harmonious features and variety of expressions.

In the short time we'd been acquainted, Amy seemed to me to be mysterious and unintelligible: either strict or modest—and sometimes absolutely without morals. Whatever expressions her face took, no matter what feeling overtook her and how she expressed it—all this she did naturally and beautifully. I feasted my eyes on her, experiencing a strange, unknown feeling, as if I had merged with this woman. Could it be that a woman makes us who we are really supposed to be? Where did I get this strange perception that I'd known her for a long time? I believed that she felt the same way I did. We were like two reincarnated savages from the Stone Age, finding ourselves in New York thousands of years later and accidentally meeting each other here.

"I also love jewelry—real jewelry; not cheap, but pieces of art," she revealed.

"I'll try to remember that. Let's go to Barnes and Noble," I offered. "They have great cappuccino in the café."

"Okay, but before that, let's go to Petco. I need to buy food for my Cupcake."

"For who?"

"Cupcake is my cat, the only friend that I really love."

After Petco, we went for a cappuccino. Then we walked around the park again. Dusk was settling in. We were probably making a tenth lap around the deserted park. We didn't want to say goodnight just yet. Amy's eyelids sparkled with silver specks in the twilight, giving her a mystical hue.

* * *

"More! More! More! Deeper! Give me your cock, Ben! I want it in my mouth! I want to deep throat your big dick! Aah! Delicious! I never sucked such a yummy dick before in my life…"

I was squeezing her big breasts tightly, biting her large nipples. Her fingers, lips, and tongue truly possessed an ancient magical power.

The moon was shining through the window. We were lying on the bed next to each other.

"My stepfather was attracted to me." Amy continued to tell me about herself, stroking her raised hands. "I'm sure he secretly wanted to fuck me, but didn't risk it, so instead he abused me so much, physically and emotionally. In response to this, I became embittered and out of control, turning from the little princess of the family into the black sheep. I could hardly wait for high school to be over, and after receiving my diploma, I immediately ran away from home and went around the country. I danced in various clubs using falsified documents, changed boyfriends, and drank a lot. I've always felt comfortable and safe under the influence of alcohol. But I didn't know any measure—I was crazy while drunk. Because of alcohol I even started having epileptic seizures, and I realized that I shouldn't drink at all." She got quiet for a short time. "I don't even know why I'm telling you all this, Ben. For some reason I just want you to know the truth about me. Few people know the whole truth about me; you can even say no one truly does. But someday millions of readers will know about me."

"What readers are you talking about?"

"I've been writing a novel."

"Really?"

"Yes. I am a writer, a unique writer, not like everyone else."

"Do you have any special education?"

"No, I don't. I planned to go to college for it but changed my mind. A true writer needs only a gift, and nothing else. I write wherever and whenever inspiration strikes me. Creativity has always been a salvation for me."

"What's this novel about?"

"I write about everything that worries me. Most importantly, this is a novel about love. True love! I thought about this for a long time and concluded that in the universe there is nothing stronger than true love. However, love is not only a blessing; love requires a lot of work, a deep humility, and an ability to always remember that you're responsible for someone you love."

"Hmm… interesting. Can I read it?"

"No, it's not completed yet and I'm still working on it. Some parts I keep in drafts on paper, some on my laptop, and some just in memory. I still must put it all together. Benji, how can I explain the main thing? See, I don't understand myself; I don't understand who I am. Sometimes it seems to me that I don't even exist on earth. I'm good at pretending, playing different roles to fit into the surroundings. But in my heart, I know very well that this is all a sham. I feel truly myself only when inspiration strikes me, and I write. But inspiration doesn't come all that often as I want."

She became silent again and we lay quietly for a long time, listening to the leaves rustling outside the window and at times to a car driving along the road, breaking the silence.

Suddenly she turned to her side, facing me.

"Tell me the truth. You must be happy to have fucked me, right? I know, all you White men want to fuck a Black woman for the novelty or allure, and then you dream up stories about how it was, how a Black bitch screams during sex so the whole neighborhood hears it, and how we jump as high as the ceiling during an orgasm. Isn't that true? Yes, it is! I *am* this Black bitch! Come to me, honey…"

* * *

In the morning, we woke up to the early chirping of birds outside the window. I took Amy to the salt marsh, which in the mornings was still deserted. She was wearing jeans, and I gave her my white T-shirt, the sleeves of which she rolled up to her elbows. She was not wearing a bra.

The air was still. We entered a grove, where in a clearing a few feral cats were devouring a snack out of plastic bowls the locals had left. We walked along a wide, winding path that stretched through the grove along the bay.

"Have you really not mastered and acquired any normal vocation in all these years?" I asked her. "I understand that writing a novel is compelling, it is salvation for you, but it's not a job. And home aide—sorry, not a vocation for such a smart woman like you."

She was embarrassed, as if I had taken her by surprise with this question.

"I have what you call a normal job. I'm a nurse. Yes, a nurse," she said, lowering her voice as if wishing no one else but me would know. "But now I don't want to talk about it. It's a very unpleasant, dark story for me. I'll tell you about it some other time. Look, a raccoon!"

We stopped by a thick bush where it was eating nuts. The raccoon was too busy eating to pay any attention to us.

In the near distance by the water there was a raised wooden post, dug into the ground and topped with a large peregrine falcon's nest. It was very difficult to approach, since prickly bushes grew everywhere and the whole area was permeated with channels created by the tides. At the beginning of summer, two falcons had hatched, and recently they'd begun to leave the nest and fly under their parents' supervision.

A birdwatcher—a middle-aged man whose chest was covered with massive binoculars and a telescope—stood on the path watching the falcons in the nest.

"Can I take a look?" Amy asked the man with a light-hearted smile, addressing him as if he were a longtime friend.

Without changing his brooding facial expression, the birdwatcher took off the binoculars and gave them to Amy.

"Two parents and two cute kids," she waved her hand, screaming. "Hey, sisters, I'm here!"

It seemed as if one of the birds had heard her cry. It darted from the nest and, soaring into the sky, screeched, "Kee-eeee-arr!" as it flew in our direction. It made several wide circles above us, and then returned to the nest.

Amy slowly lowered the binoculars. She stood frozen, wide-eyed.

"Are you okay?" I asked, a little worried.

But she was silent, remaining still. Then she turned her face toward me. It bore an expression of surprise, even inexplicable fear.

"The soul of a bird has now entered me. I've become a bird, a falcon!"

I silently nodded, not daring to contradict her. I realized that she wasn't joking and believed what she said.

Oddly, as if to confirm her words, a gray-brown falcon's feather slowly descended from above and lay on the ground in front of us.

"See?! Do you see? Jesus Christ!" Amy picked up the feather and carefully examined it in front of her face.

We continued on our way. Soon we found ourselves on the beach. The water was crystal clear, so much so that it was possible to discern even the eyes of fingerlings swimming near a tuft of grass.

"I'd like to swim," said Amy.

"I've never seen people swim here," I remarked, and it was true.

"Well, I'll be the first." Without saying a word, she swiftly took off her T-shirt and then her sneakers. Unbuttoning the zipper, she pulled off her jeans. "Hold these."

She gave me her clothes and smiled—clearly catching my eye sliding up and down her beautiful naked body and her white panties, which also quickly slid down her hips and wound up in my hands.

I watched as she went along the water's edge, her bottom slightly twitching.

At that moment, standing on the beach watching her, I realized I knew absolutely nothing about her. Currently a home attendant, former stripper, writer. Also, a nurse with a dark history. How could all this be combined into one person? Who is she really, this woman?

Meanwhile, Amy stopped and turned to face the water. After standing for a short time, she raised her hands to the sky, flapped them like wings, and suddenly screamed loudly, "Kee-eeee-arr!"

PART TWO

First Offer

A few weeks later, Amy and I were approaching the building where I lived. My neighbors sat on the bench nearby—old grandpas and grannies, gossiping about one thing or another.

Pleasant old folks, some of whom I had already gotten acquainted with. They had been living in this building for a decade. Their children had grown up and gone to live elsewhere. They were very happy that a young, new shareholder moved into the building. The men invite me to play bingo with them on Thursdays at the "casino" located in the basement, and still pester me to become a member of the "men's club." Despite their old age and frail health, they're still hanging on. They're on the board of the co-op, still holding all the reins of governance in their hands.

Amy disliked them. She believed they viewed her as a "woman from the ghetto."

After greeting the neighbors, Amy and I entered the building.

"Get ready to hear some amazing news! I spoke to my boss today, the ER director at the hospital, and told him about you," I said, opening the door of my apartment and letting Amy enter ahead of me.

"Did you forget, Ben? I told you what happened when I worked as a nurse and began selling pills. I got busted, and my nursing license was suspended." From a candlestick that stood on a shelf among trinkets, she picked up the falcon feather from the marsh she had asked me to save. Stopping by the mirror, she began caressing her cheek and neck with it waiting for me to continue.

"Yes, you told me. You can't work as a nurse yet because your license is still suspended. But you can still do something else, as a clerk, for example. It's better than being a home health aide, right? Alexa, play 'Whisky Bar' by the Doors," I said, taking off my shoes.

"And what did your boss say?" Amy still held the feather as she watched her reflection in the mirror.

"My boss said, 'If we don't find another whisky bar, I tell you we must die, I tell you, I tell you...'" I sang in unison with Jim Morrison. "He'll hire you to work in the registration office. Prepare your résumé, and I'll take it to the HR department." I went up to her and placed my hands on her hips.

She pondered for a moment, as if scrolling through all the possible obstacles which could prevent her from obtaining this job.

"I guess it could work."

She began to lightly stroke my face and my throat with the feather, and I lifted my chin, closed my eyes, and purred like a cat.

Kaddish

My father and I were sitting at an outside table at a café. I was drinking coffee, and he had a Coke. Coffee wasn't his drink of choice.

"Amy told me you're going to get her a new job at your hospital. Is that right?" My father smoothed out his thin, gray, brushed-back hair.

"Yes, hopefully they'll hire her."

My father patted himself on the front pockets of his jeans. "Fuck, I haven't smoked in three months, but my hands automatically go looking for a cigarette and a lighter. We're slaves of our habits."

"It seems you're not happy that she's leaving you soon."

"A bit. Even though she has a bold personality and sometimes can go the entire day just reading stupid love stories, she knows how to care for the weak and feeble. Unfortunately, I still belong to this category. Anyway, it's not a big deal. This one leaves, another one comes. This is not a wife, just some common home aide, a common Black bitch."

"Goodbye, Dad, I'm going," I said while standing up.

"Alright, alright, my bad," he mumbled with some guilt in his voice, grabbing my arm. "Don't go. You're so hotheaded." He held onto me until I reluctantly sat down. "Honestly, Ben, I didn't expect that you and her would form a serious relationship. I wish you'd go back to Sarah and Veronica instead. Do you keep in contact with them?"

"No, practically never."

"That's too bad. Don't get offended, but your Amy is not as naive as she seems at first glance. Don't be a loco. She's very cunning and greedy, like all former strippers."

"What makes you think she was a stripper?"

"Son, I'm ashamed to say that I used to spend more time in strip clubs than I did with you when you were a kid. I can see right through them. Your Amy is a professional; she knows how to get money out of men, as all good strippers do, and Black girls do it far better than Whites. Why don't you sit down and calculate how much money you've already spent on her—on Uber, cafés, cosmetics, and other female crap. Then try to remember if she has ever given you a cent back. Are you silent? You see? You know I'm right."

There was a short pause. My dad smoothed his hair again and, raising his head, looked out into the distance.

"A lot has changed for me lately, Ben. During my life, I saved some money. I have two streams of income—one from the union and one from Social Security. Plus, a 401(k). On the other hand, unfortunately, for the third year in a row I have been living alone. At first, I thought that if I became single, I'd quickly be able to find another woman. But that didn't come to fruition. I don't need old women, and young ones don't need me. Had I been, say, ten years younger, it might have been a different story, but I'm 75. Ugh!"

We kept silent for a while.

"Listen, son. Let's choose a day to visit your mother's grave," he said unexpectedly. "I haven't been there since her death."

* * *

I took a day off from work, and that morning we left
for the cemetery. My father wanted to drive, so we took
his Grand Cherokee. It was important to him as a sign that
he was getting back in shape. He worked as a driver for
almost thirty years, first driving a truck, then a bus in a ye-
shiva, so, understandably, he could drive a car with his
eyes closed. However, his age made itself known. I noticed
it today, while we were in the car. Sometimes, he'd brake
too suddenly, change lanes hesitantly, and even a few times
didn't use a turn signal, which he always considered to be
the behavior of a typical Brooklyn prick. Just as before, he
often swore at other drivers who either cut in front of him or
changed lanes without signaling. "Schmuck! Why don't you
use your signal? Oh, you idiot, look at how you're driving!"

We got to our destination, drove through the open gate,
and at low speed, the car rolled along a bumpy asphalt road.
I didn't even have to tell him the way—he had a brilliant
topographic memory. He turned wherever necessary, even
though the meandering road was quite confusing. Initially
after my mother's death, it took me a lot of effort not to get
lost. Meanwhile, he'd been here just once.

"We're here." He pressed on the brake.

It was a warm autumn day. There were no other visitors.
Only a jeep with a trailer half-filled with dry leaves and
branches stood nearby, and near it two workers in uniform
smoked and were deep in loud conversation about something.

My father took out two black yarmulkes from the glove
compartment, handing one to me while putting the other
on his head and pressing it slightly. He did not believe in

God—one of his favorite expressions was, "By God, I do not believe in God." He would always chuckle while saying this, clearly finding the expression witty and funny. Now looking at him with a yarmulke covering his gray head, with sparse hair at the edges and tufts of hair in his ears, with thick eyebrows and a gloomy, frozen stare, I involuntarily thought that my father would be right at home inside a synagogue with a Torah in his hands.

We went down to the gray granite stone, under which my mother had been resting for two years. The mournful inscription on it was carved in English and ancient Hebrew, with a seven-branched candlestick and the Star of David carved over her name.

Nearby, a red rosebush grew. It was planted on the next grave, which also appeared here two years ago where some Russian-Jewish lady was buried. I noticed many European Jews don't strictly follow Jewish religious rules and plant bushes and flowers in the cemetery. During this time, the bush had grown, and its buds reached over to my mother's stone.

My father stood in front of the stone and again straightened the yarmulke on his head. Then he folded his arms and let out a deep sigh. I stood over to the side, looking at the stone and then at my father in front of it.

In an instant, my whole childhood and adolescence flashed before me. I saw pots full of soup, the most delicious soup on earth, which my mother had cooked, and dishes with stuffed fish. I remembered the weekends when we as a family went to relax at Prospect Park and how we packed the umbrellas and mats in the trunk when going to the beach at Coney Island.

A strange murmuring snapped me out of it: "Yis-gadal v`yis-kadash `sh`may raboh…"

I looked and listened more closely—it was my father whispering a prayer! The Kaddish! I knew these words. I knew them by heart. For a year after my mother's death, I went to the synagogue, which was located near where I lived at the time. Every morning at six o'clock, men gathered there and prayed, wearing tallits. I also went there. The rabbi at my mother's funeral had advised me to go to the synagogue for a year and read the Kaddish for my mother. There in the prayer hall, I was given a book where prayers were written in two languages, English and Hebrew, and instructed which page to read at which point during the service. I didn't always follow these instructions—I'd simply leaf through the prayer book and read a prayer I'd come across. They typically delved into the hidden meaning of how the Almighty created man and the people of Israel, and what hopes He had for these people. My arm would be wrapped in a thin leather black strap called a tefillin, and a black wooden box was attached to my forehead with another tefillin. Inside the box was a piece of paper bearing the words of the sacred prayer "Shema, Yisrael!" During these prayers, it seemed to me that my mother was with me; that she had not gone anywhere and never died but simply changed the form of her existence so she would never part with me again.

"Yis-gadal v`yis-kadash `sh`may raboh…" were the words of the Kaddish, which I read according to tradition before the end of the service. All the praying men in the synagogue looked at me with respect and sympathy, since everyone knew why I was there and the extent of my grief.

"Yis-gadal v`yis-kadash `sh`may raboh…" My father spoke softly, shaking his gray head slightly, and I began to utter with him the unforgettable words of the Kaddish.

I wasn't sure how much time passed, but it felt like an eternity.

"That's all. We did a good deed. At the same time, we breathed some fresh air with the dead," my father said, finishing the prayer and chuckling.

After this stupid joke, a rush of anger suddenly gripped me—anger toward this manner of his to say what is necessary and then what is not necessary, toward his buffoonery, and toward his ability to spoil everything. Sitting down, I began to collect leaves and fallen rose petals lying on the ground near the grave into a plastic bag. I didn't want to look at my father right now. I thought that going with him to my mother's grave would allow me to forgive him. Yet, I still felt in my soul a vast ocean of hatred toward him.

We were driving back home on the same highway. Now it was full of cars, and we were stuck in traffic.

"It turns out that we both know the Kaddish. Once upon a time, I read it for my father in the synagogue, although, by God, I do not believe in God," my father said, looking in the rearview mirror. "I remember the rabbi told me at the time that there is no greater misfortune for a Jew than if his son wouldn't read the Kaddish for him after his death." He frowned. Something was obviously bothering him, and he was pale. It even seemed to me that he was not physically well now.

Finally, we got to the street where I lived. He stopped the car near my building. I thought that I should invite him in since he'd never been to my new apartment, but I didn't want to.

"Go on, Ben. I need to go to the pharmacy to get some medicine," he said, as if reading my mind. "And you know what?" He suddenly put his hand on my shoulder.

"What?" I tensed up. I didn't remember when he'd soberly, calmly, and warmly put his hand on my shoulder in such a way.

He gently drew me toward him, and I felt his cheeks with their rough, bristled hair on my face.

Rumblings

One day in the ER, I was sitting with Dr. Mercy in our office, working on our computers. He was so busy that he didn't even have time to tell me one of his war stories from the army.

The silence in the office would sometimes be disrupted when our boss, Dr. Michael Harris, would occasionally rush in and lash out at Dr. Mercy with terrible language.

"Adam, what the fuck?! Why didn't you tell me about this?"

"Shit! I didn't know about it," Dr. Mercy would respond.

Dr. Harris had been well acquainted with Dr. Mercy for many years, so in their private conversations they didn't care much about using foul language.

Finally, the shift was almost over. The boss left, and Dr. Mercy and I prepared to leave as well.

"Michael is a great guy, outgoing and forgiving. But sometimes he's very hard to bear," said Dr. Mercy grudgingly. "He's like this today because they had a closed meeting of the hospital's administration where they were discussing some important news—I guess not good news. By the way, have you noticed that in recent weeks we've had an unusual number of Chinese patients in the ER?"

"Now that you mention it, indeed, there has been an increase in the number of Chinese patients lately. I wonder why."

"They all have the same symptoms: breathing problems, fever, and weakness. We admit them with a diagnosis of shortness of breath or pneumonia, but I think it's something else." He got up, zipped up his jacket, and with a thoughtful look, repeated, "Yes, it's something entirely different. Something we've never dealt with before."

Witch

"**W**ell, I just knew it." Amy poured seltzer water into an empty glass and drank it in one gulp.

"Why didn't you tell me about it before? I thought you only had a suspended nursing license, but you're also on probation! Naturally hospitals don't hire people with open criminal cases. HR did a full criminal background check on you."

"I was hoping that it wouldn't turn up; that it would somehow slip through."

"I understand. I've already established that it's the philosophy of your life — 'Maybe, somehow, I'll slip through. Maybe no one will find out. Maybe I'll get lucky,'" I said in a moral tone, emphasizing the word *maybe*.

She suddenly frowned. "Don't talk to me that way! I'm not your wife. Yes, I did some crap. But I paid the price for this. You can't even imagine what I had to go through then!" She was furious, but tears appeared in her eyes.

"I apologize for my tone. Sorry. Today I looked like an idiot when my boss called me in and was upset. He was counting on you to work in the ER's registration office. I didn't even know what to say to him."

Amy nodded and stared at me questioningly, as if she were seeking permission to do something.

"Do you have any wine, Ben?" She raised the same glass out of which she had just drunk seltzer water and extended her hand toward me. "Pour me, I want to get drunk."

I shook my head no.

"Ben, pleeeease."

"No."

"Fuck!" She put the empty glass on the marble counter-top with such force that I was surprised that it didn't shatter. She was about to burst into tears.

"Calm down, it's not the end of the world. It didn't work out for you the first time, but it will the next. Let's go for a walk in the salt marsh. There are birds and cats waiting for you."

* * *

It was still light out, but the yellow moon was becoming clearer in the sky. We walked along a wide dirt path that curled around the bay. Its smooth surface was no longer disturbed by the boats that had entered it during the sum-mer. In the distance, on the opposite bank, dark dots mov-ing close to each other were visible—probably a flock of gray ducks looking for food by the shore.

"New York is a cold city. All the years I've lived here, and I still can't get used to your rough climate, which doesn't compare to the soft climate in Georgia. 'Keeping Georgiaaa on my mind'," Amy finished by singing Ray Charles' famous song.

"Yeah," I replied, inhaling with joy the smells of the damp earth and drying leaves.

It was not windy near the house, but here, in the open space of the marsh, the wind came in bursts, blowing the cold right underneath my jacket. Despite this, Amy and I decided to walk the entire route and made a wide circle along the marsh.

Twilight was creeping in from the horizon, but the high pole with the falcon's nest was still faintly visible. It was already the end of fall; the chicks had fledged, grown up, and flown away, and the nest was empty until next spring.

Amy stared at the empty nest, then waved her hands and screamed.

"Hey, sisters! I'm here! C'mon!"

There was no response to her cry. We kept walking.

There were no birds chirping, as if they were all hiding somewhere. Occasionally a lonely crow with its dreary "caw" flew in from somewhere and sat on a bare branch. It seemed as if the salt marsh had become lifeless — abandoned and unwanted.

"Did you hear about a new epidemic in China?" I asked. "It's not clear what kind of virus it is. I hope it doesn't come here."

"I hope so. Let's walk faster; it's chilly." Amy shrugged her shoulders from the cold and, throwing a hood over her head, picked up her pace.

* * *

During the night I was awakened by strange sounds, as if the wings of a bird were flapping around nearby. When I looked closely, I saw a moving dark spot on the windowsill. What is it? I thought. A squirrel? Or a bat? But how did it get here? Did it chew through the screen in the window? However, the window is closed. Did it get in from some crack? I strained my eyes, trying to see who it was.

"Kee-eeeee-arr!" There was a shrill cry, and whatever was on the windowsill jumped up and began to fly across the room, bumping into the closet, the lamp, and the mirror. I turned on the lamp on my nightstand.

It was a young peregrine falcon, perhaps one of those that had hatched from the nest at the salt marsh this summer. But for some reason, it didn't fly away for the winter with its brethren. The bird kept striking the mirror, gliding down the glass while trying to catch itself on something, and was still desperately screaming.

It was unbearable to watch. I got out of bed and opened the window. Then I gently grabbed the bird by the wings to release it out the window. But as I did, the falcon began to peck me with its hooked beak, leaving bloody wounds on my wrists, chest, and stomach.

"Aaah!" I screamed in pain and…woke up!

I was frightened and hadn't yet fully come to my senses. I ran my hand over the crumpled blanket near me to feel Amy's warm body—but she was gone!

It was dark. The door to the living room was closed, but a faint light came through the gap. As I rose, adjusting my underwear and stroking my wrists and chest as if there were fresh wounds on them, I quietly opened the door and walked down the corridor to the living room. I stopped at the doorstep.

Amy sat at the table, wearing a short-sleeved black T-shirt and black panties, with one leg over the other. She was writing something on a piece of paper lying in front of her on the table. She frowned, bit her lip, and bulged out her big eyes. She was breathing heavily, her breasts heaving under her T-shirt. At times, she squeezed her free left hand into a fist so tightly that it seemed that her fingers would crack. Her whole face seemed to be bloated and looked somewhat scary.

A witch! A real witch! I thought unwillingly.

"Benny? Is that you? Why aren't you sleeping?" She raised her head and looked at me.

I shrugged.

"Do you want to hear some of it?" she asked excitedly. Without waiting for my response, she took the sheet of paper with words scribbled all over it and, bringing it slightly closer to her face, began to read expressively. "Life is the Word. This Word lives in me. It is conceived in me, deep in my uterus, where it grows and yearns to express itself through me. The Word gradually becomes me, and I it. It flows through me, into me, and out of me; it flows like a river, like an eternal inexhaustible source, drawing everything in, both the living and dead. God created me only to conceive and express the living Word through me." Taking a short pause, she turned the page over and, sighing deeply, continued. "Thanks to the Word, I've become a shining star, a heavy stone, and a light bird. Yes, I'm becoming a falcon—a falcon soaring through the autumn sky! I'm flyyying!" She waved with her free hand as if it were a wing and continued to smoothly make the motion to the rhythm of her reading. "The southwest wind picks me up and carries me upward. I'm floating in a current of air, in a deep blue ocean of air. My heart becomes covered in flesh, fuzz, and feathers. The air flows lift me higher and higher. Closing my large, hooked beak, I look with my sharp, yellow eye in the direction of the blue ridges of Georgia, appearing faintly in the haze. I want to fly there, but the rising stream of air lifts me even

higher. The sacs of my lungs compress from lack of air. I'm so carried away! I feel anger mixed with the horror of freedom. A shrill cry breaks out of my chest—'Kee-eeeee-arr!'"
After making the loud scream of the falcon, Amy fell silent, putting her palm with spread fingers on the marble countertop. Her chest was heaving, as if she were still engulfed in the dense layers of the atmosphere.

"You're a witch, a talented witch," I whispered, getting closer to take her in my arms.

She turned to face me and, while laughing, suddenly shoved me hard in the chest. I played along, pretending to lose my balance, and fell to the floor. Lunging from her chair, Amy fell on top of me. She thrust her sharp nails into my chest and whispered, "Now I'm going to peck at your heart."

* * *

On the weekend, we went to the famed Cotton Club in Harlem. Jazz musicians performed there. We sat at one of the tables and ordered food as we listened to the music.

That evening, Amy looked like a queen. She was wearing a tight, bright-red dress that was just below the knees, and black tights with silver sequins. She had put her newly reddish hair in an afro.

She was flying high, and certainly the center of attention. She sang along with the singers, danced, and participated in conversations with the audience and musicians during breaks.

Looking at her, admiring her, I realized that I was completely losing my head and falling in love with this woman even more.

PART THREE

New Nostradamus

Every morning, as usual, the team of medical staff made their rounds in the ER and listened to the nurses' short reports on each patient. I listened more carefully to the information. If before I was only interested in those from the yellow gown zone, now I wanted to know about everyone else.

The virus had already spread beyond China, crossed the ocean, and was roaming across America. The number of COVID-19 deaths in the United States was already in the thousands. The news reported that some lawyer had recently returned to New York from a conference in China and then went to a meeting with colleagues in Manhattan. According to the latest data, he had infected more than fifty people at once! It sounded somewhat shocking that one person at one meeting could do that. The consolation was that it happened in Manhattan. We lived in Brooklyn, so maybe we wouldn't be affected.

But soon we did start getting the first patients properly diagnosed with COVID-19. Initially, those suspected of having it were placed in special isolated single-bed rooms. The influx of people increased measurably every day. And it wasn't just the sick arriving with COVID symptoms. Frightened, vulnerable, and confused people also came. They already knew about COVID but did not yet understand what to do and how to escape from it, so they came to the hospital. We advised them to leave as soon as possible, because the hospital was becoming a more dangerous place because of the high risk of infection. Not everyone was cooperative. Sometimes we had to ask the hospital police for help to escort them out. Some swore and threatened to sue, demanding to be left in the hospital. There were even those who, in protest, just lay down on the floor in the middle of the hallways. The police would take them by the arms and legs and drag them on the floor to the exit.

Dr. Mercy now spent most of his time not in the office but inside the department. He walked through the corridors of the ER with a heavy gait. The power, energy, and determination of this former military man were apparent in how he carried himself. Nurses, residents, and caseworkers all approached him to ask about certain patients. Without stopping, he gave immediate orders to send this patient to the psych unit, another to cardiology, and yet another home. "Let him get discharged; get him out of here right now."

Looking at him at such moments, I imagined the afterlife, where we'll all presumably end up after death and meet God. Perhaps God is not at all how we imagine Him—sitting majestically on a heavenly throne. Maybe God is up there intently walking through celestial corridors, and, like Dr. Mercy, He barks out commands to the angels about each newcomer. "This one goes to paradise, this one to purgatory, and that one to hell; get this fuck to hell right now."

Dr. Harris, as the director of the ER, now had a lot of meetings with staff and appeared in all corners of the department. The situation was changing by the minute; it was necessary to make a decision immediately. His demeanor began to change. He was now unnaturally calm. He was saving his mental energy, as if he knew he'd soon need it in unprecedented quantities.

"Ben, do you want to know how I imagine the foreseeable future because of the pandemic?" Dr. Harris asked me. "I have an idea, just listen: Sickness and death will sharply spike. The economy will drain. Then, inevitably, crime will jump. Our civilization will head down." He pointed his thumb down to the floor. "In short, fucking Armageddon."

"Doctor, you sound like Nostradamus."

"I hear your sarcasm, my friend. Let's come back to this conversation in a few weeks."

Jealousy

Amy asked me to drive up to her house to take her cat to the vet. She described its condition in such a tragic tone that it touched my heart, and I worked straight through lunch to leave early so we could get it examined.

Amy felt offended when anyone viewed her as a "woman from the ghetto," but because of recent professional and financial calamity, she was forced to move into one of the Brooklyn "ghettos" (or, speaking in less-offensive language, underdeveloped neighborhood.) I'd been there a couple of times before to get my car fixed. But that was before the pandemic, and I didn't know if anything had changed there since then.

As I was driving slowly through the streets, my Nissan was tossed on bumps and potholes; many roads here were dug up and traffic was blocked due to the construction. There was work going on for installation pipelines to several buildings. Most likely, this project was conceived and started prior to the pandemic. Now it was extremely difficult to figure out how to get to the right address—which road was blocked off to traffic and which was not. Giant jackhammers from the towering cranes and construction machinery were driving piles into the ground and laying concrete blocks. Where work was going on, everything rattled and jangled, and smoke and soot hung in the air.

On other streets it was eerily quiet. There was litter, and in some places, people had clearly thrown trash out of garbage cans directly onto the ground. Here and there, by the fences and house walls, people sat on crates, smoking weed, drinking vodka and beer as they loudly argued. At one point, I drove past a homeless camp, where blankets, mattresses, clothes, and even utensils and gas stoves were lying on the ground. The people, of different ages and skin color, but mostly Blacks, also drank beer and vodka and smoked weed to the blast of a stereo.

I was amazed at the number of broken windows in parked cars—it was impossible not to notice. They were on almost every street and everywhere on the sidewalk small pieces of broken glass lay scattered.

During the entire drive, I saw only one police car.

I unwittingly remembered Dr. Harris's recent words that because of the pandemic our civilization would go down. "Fucking Armageddon." I laughed at his words then and with some sarcasm called him Nostradamus. At the time, I thought doctors understood life solely from the angle of physiology: yes, they can make extraordinary decisions regarding the right treatment, but once they move outside the box of physiology and medicine into the realm of politics and culture, they start thinking with clichés and stereotypes. But here, just a month passed, and the first signs of Armageddon were evident in front of my eyes!

* * *

After some time, I was sitting on a small sofa in Amy's studio on the second floor, watching her getting dressed.

"What's going on in your ER? A lot of sick people coming in?" she asked, putting on her panties and then wool sweatpants, which had come off of her shortly before, not without my help.

"Yes, every day there are more and more patients."

"Do you wear a mask in there?" Slightly bending her knees and squatting, she pulled up her pants to the waist.

This gesture of her pulling up her sweatpants, slightly squatting, made me freeze for a moment. It reminded me of my mother. She, just like Amy now, pulled up her sweatpants the same way, and for some reason I always found it fascinating.

"Yes, I try to wear a mask. But it's hard to get one. They're only given to doctors and nurses, and only one per shift. All the other staff members protect themselves as best they can. Some wrap their faces with bandanas or scarves, some wear goggles, and someone came in wearing a motorcycle helmet," I answered, getting up and taking my jeans from the chair.

"Are you serious?"

"Absolutely. Our ER now resembles a circus. Today, a gift came from Home Depot—they donated 50 special protective shields, the kind carpenters use. I helped bring them into the ER."

"Who would have imagined that we'd find ourselves in a situation worse than in some third world countries?" Amy put a dark jumper over her head and began to comb her hair.

Meanwhile, I walked across the old parquet floor, which creaked under the weight of my medium-build body as if an elephant was walking on it.

The studio where Amy lived consisted of one room connected to a kitchen. The ceiling — once white, now gray — was covered in small cracks, as were the walls. In general, it was clean, but not ideally organized.

"What are you thinking?" I asked, seeing how Amy was suddenly staring at some point on the wall, standing motionless.

"Oh, nothing…it's a shame I can't do anything as a nurse right now. I have a nursing education and some experience, and I could be useful. But I can't! By the way, they say that Blacks are more susceptible to COVID than Whites, with higher death rates."

"I'm not sure. We have ER patients in serious condition, no matter the race."

"You just don't pay attention to the fact that there are more Blacks," she said in a confident tone of voice." Okay, it's time to go. Cupcake, come here baby." The whole time the cat lay on the soft mat under the table. She took the cat in her arms, pinning it to her chest. "My poor baby, come to mommy. We're gonna go to the doctor, who will take care of you. Don't cry, don't cry." She kissed the cat on the face.

This gave me an unpleasant reaction, as I would have to kiss her right after she kissed her cat. I have never liked cats; I didn't like their smell, and deep inside my heart for some unknown reason I was even a little afraid of them.

I was also annoyed that it was cold in the room, and it was a shame that Amy lived in such poor conditions.

Meanwhile, she moved the plastic cage with her foot and put the cat inside. She took her hooded jacket from the hanger and announced, "I'm ready! What's going on, Ben?"

I was standing in front of her old short dresser, looking at the framed photos. Amy was in different places and with different people. I liked the picture of her in a provocative bikini on the beach, hugging a young woman her age, maybe her friend. I also liked the picture where she's hugging an elderly woman in a chair, probably her mother. But I didn't like the picture of her profile, kissing a young Black man in a white T-shirt with a white cap on his head, slightly shifted backward.

"Why should I stay hungry all day and work through lunch for your cat? You didn't even offer me anything to eat." I said, turning to her. I was starting to get flushed with anger, blood surging to my temples. So, she is dating me, but keeps *his* picture!

"It's your jailbird, right?" I pointed at the photo.

"Why are you so jealous, Ben? Yes, that's Jason, my boyfriend. I told you about him. He'll be released from jail in a year or sooner."

"I wish this convict stays there forever!"

"Don't say such stupid things. You don't even know what kind of person he is," her eyes shone with some evil spark. She pushed a strand of hair off her forehead. "So, are we going to the vet or not?"

"I'm not sure. First, I'm starving and want to eat. And secondly, I want you to get rid of this picture."

"Oh, is that how it's gonna be?" She went over, picked up the picture, and kissed it several times. "My sweetie Jason. You know how much I miss you and how much my hot pussy misses you." Then she put the photo back and stood before me, with her hands on her lower back. "How do you like this?"

I snorted from anger. "If one more word fly out of your mouth…"

At that moment, everything in the apartment shook. Apparently, below the street, a giant pile was being driven into the ground. After every blow, from the roof to the foundation, the whole four-story house shook so much that it seemed like the next one would crash down. Dishes rattled on Amy's kitchen table. Her shoes, roller skates, and cans of cat food jumped on the floor.

Turning around, with one giant sweep, I knocked all the framed pictures from her dresser to the floor. "To hell with it!" I headed for the front door, tearing my jacket from the hanger, and slammed it behind me. I ran down the stairs to my car.

"Don't call me anymore!" I heard Amy's voice from the window above.

But I didn't look back. I was walking straight ahead.

Flash Point

"**B**en, it's me."

"I see that it's you. What happened?" I asked my father, hearing his muffled but still strong voice on my cell phone. I sat at my desk in the office.

"Here's the thing…" He hesitated somewhat, as if not knowing how to explain the situation.

It was strange to me—here was my all-knowing father at a loss as to how best to explain himself. As long as I've known him, he's always expressed himself quickly, sometimes too quickly. Because he often jumps to conclusions, he says whatever comes to mind, and worst of all, he could purposefully or unwittingly be offensive.

From the time I was a child, in conversations with me, my dad was typically rude and rarely listened to what I was saying. I remember sometimes I'd be telling him something important to me. He seemed to listen, nodding, and then out of the blue interrupted me, asking about something completely different. It became clear to me that he wasn't listening to me at all and didn't care what I said. He rarely let me speak my mind; as a rule, he gave orders and instructions, with no room for discussion.

I was always just a "dummy" and "loco" to him.

And so, since I had lately gotten close to him again after his heart surgeries, I noticed a certain strangeness to him. The all-knowing cloak came off, and his manner of giving orders had changed considerably. I noticed that before saying something, he sometimes hesitated and pondered, as if trying to find the right words to express his thoughts. This didn't happen often, but it did undeniably happen.

"There's a certain situation with Amy," he said. "She's not how she usually is today. Her face is puffy and she's trembling, as if she's ill. Maybe she has the virus?"

"Where is she now?"

"She is here. I gave her two Tylenols, as she asked. I think we should call 911. But she doesn't want to go to the hospital."

"Don't do anything. Wait for me; I'll come there soon."

Shortly afterward, I was racing into Bay Ridge on the highway along the Hudson. I was speeding at 70 miles per hour, passing cars.

"Why the hell am I going to save her? Why should I care? Let her wait for her jailbird," I repeated to myself.

But in my heart, of course, I was glad that I would finally see her, because I missed her terribly.

"Where is she?" I asked my father when he opened the door.

"Here, in the living-room. It's a good thing you came. She's been gone for four days, but she's here today. Look at the condition she's in." My father was babbling, following behind me.

Amy was lying on the sofa with her legs to her stomach and her hands pinned to her chest. She was staring straight ahead with eyes wide open. Saliva trickled down from the corner of her half-open mouth. She was shaking. Stains covered her gray wool pants. In front of the sofa on the floor were her white dirty sneakers.

"I don't know what's wrong with her. She came in the morning; she was more or less fine except for a headache. But after a couple of hours, she became like this." My father continued speaking, walking up to her. "I see you're not getting better, only worse. We should call 911."

"I don't want to go to any hospital. I'll feel better soon, and I'll go home."

"What hurts?" I asked, taking a step toward her, though I already knew perfectly well what was wrong with her and why she was in such a state.

"My belly. And it's hard to breathe. I have a splitting headache," she replied, not even glancing at me. "I feel so horrible that I think I am going to die. I see strange lights and some white spots in the distance. I'm afraid; I'm full of fear…"

"Bring water, quickly," I ordered my dad.

From my jeans pocket, I pulled out two packets with red, elongated pills which I had taken from the ER. Separating the corner foil with my nail, I tore off the cover and put two tablets on my palm.

"Here, take them." I helped Amy to get up in order to take the pills while my father gave her a glass of water to chase them down.

"What is it?" she asked.

"Don't worry about it, just take it."

I held her from the back by the neck, leaning slightly toward her. I was struck by the sharp, foul stench that usually comes from alcoholics.

I felt that my heart was about to break from guilt. Amy must have started drinking because of me after that stupid jealousy scene in her apartment that I created. Yes, of course — when I stormed out, she drank for four days straight!

"Now you'll feel better. Just try to hang in there," I said, carefully laying her onto her back. "Yes, there are a lot of COVID patients in all the hospitals right now, so I don't think that's the best option. We can handle it ourselves. Here's the plan: I'll bring enough pills from the hospital to last a week. I know how to open some doors in the Pyxis where we store the drugs."

She smiled faintly. "You're going to steal pills from the hospital for me? Look, be careful that you don't get busted and stripped of your license, like me."

"Don't worry. Dad, she'll stay with you till this evening. I'm going back to work now, since I only took leave for an hour. After work, I'll come back and we'll decide what to do next, okay?" I spoke in a commanding tone. I mentally noted that now I speak to my father just as he once did with me; or rather, I don't listen but give *him* orders. How quickly our roles have changed in life!

"Do you want to get up?" I asked Amy, seeing that she had sat up on the sofa with her legs dangling.

"Yes, I need to go to the bathroom." She got up.

"She's cold. Get another plaid blanket out of the closet for her," I told my father, looking at the clock. "Alright, I have to go. I'll be back soon."

She nodded. Suddenly, she extended her arms toward me.

"Benji! Aaah!!!" With a cry, she collapsed on the floor.

For a few moments, she was kneeling in front of me, and I couldn't understand what was wrong with her. I even had a thought that she was playing a stupid penance scene. But a few seconds later, when she rolled over on her back, I understood what was going on. Seizure! Her arms and legs were shaking in spasms, and her whole body twisted, as if someone was torturing her from the inside. Her face became distorted, and white foam oozed from her mouth.

"Hr-hr-hr…" Amy wheezed.

I fell on my knees in front of her.

"My dear, my sweetheart. Don't. Don't," I whispered, crawling in front of her on my knees and not taking my eyes off her convulsed face. "I will never again ever harm you. I swear, swear…"

* * *

We were driving in the car, on the same highway, but now in the opposite direction—toward my hospital. We were in my father's car, which was bigger and more spacious than mine. My dad was driving, while Amy and I were in the back seat. She was lying down, with her head on my knees. I silently stroked her cheek. She had already regained her senses a little, staring at me with half-open, cloudy eyes.

"You know, before I lost consciousness, I saw something strange and terrible: a fiery chariot with prophets and angels. I was in such a state, it was as if inspiration descended upon me, but so strong that I couldn't bear it."

We drove up to the ER entrance. My dad stopped the car, got out, and opened the back door. I helped Amy out and, taking her by the arm, took her inside the building.

We slowly approached the front desk check-in.

Suddenly, she freed her hand from mine. "I don't want to go there."

"Why?" I asked, stopping.

"Because this will go on my record—it'll become known to the Board of Nursing, and then I won't get my license back."

"No one will find out anything, and if they do, to hell with them! I'm sorry, but you're not a nurse, you're an idiot if you're thinking about this nonsense right now. You can have another fit any minute, even worse than the first one; it could be life-threatening."

"You're right, I know it…Listen, you've already seen what a shit hole I live in, now you'll see me in the dimwit zone with a yellow gown on me. Lord, I might die from shame."

I became numb from her vulnerable appearance. My heart was overcome with tenderness for her. Without saying a word, I picked Amy up in my arms.

Behind the high glass partition of the front desk, a young clerk name Jessica was sitting with her mouth open with surprise, watching the whole "romantic scene." I nodded to Jessica, and she nodded understandingly in response and pressed a special button. Immediately, the automatic doors to the ER opened wide in front of me, and I carefully carried Amy inside as if she were a precious vessel.

* * *

"I've become completely blind; I don't see the obvious. For some reason, I thought it was COVID, damn it! Then, hell knows, I thought she was pregnant," my dad confessed to me as we drove home from the hospital later that night. "It turned out she was just drinking. Ugh!"

"Don't worry, Dad. You did everything right," I consoled him. "The main thing is that it turned out well. She'll be in the ward for a day or two to make sure everything's okay."

"You've turned into a professional," my dad praised. "I saw how you treated her at home today—one, two, three—everything very precise, no panic. Good job."

"Of course, Dad; I have a wonderful personal learning experience dealing with drunkards, thanks to you. Did you forget that you used to drink like a fish? I don't know how that woman of yours managed to get you to stop drinking."

"Yes, it's true, I used to drink. But never to the extent your Amy did."

"Sure, you never did," I replied with sarcasm.

My dad looked at me from the corner of his eye and chuckled, but he said nothing.

PART FOUR

Armageddon Coming

The sky over the city was cloudy; darkness was coming from everywhere and seemed about ready to absorb wonderful New York.

For me personally, one of the obvious signs that the deep foundations of our lives had been impacted and that the tectonic layers of our social existence had shifted was the appearance of beaten homeless people in the ER. Of course, even before the pandemic there were homeless in the ER. Most often, they came in themselves to "rest" from the hardships of their existence, to eat and sleep. Sometimes those folks would appear with bruises or a bloodied face—usually after falling from too much alcohol or because they'd gotten into a drunken fight.

But since the epidemic had intensified, our ER began to see wounded and crippled homeless people daily. EMTs would bring them in, usually after a call from a passerby. Many of these unfortunate souls had been subjected to brutal violence, to the point it was difficult for them to move, speak, and even breathe. It was obvious they weren't robbed—they had virtually nothing as it was—but just beaten for the hell of it. A new phase of "Armageddon" had begun with a spree of violence and debauchery.

There was no space for the homeless in the ER, which no longer had divisions. There were no "zones" anymore. Now, admitted patients were taken any place there was room: COVID patients, demented elderly, people in cardiac arrest, alcoholics in withdrawal, stroke victims, and suicidal people were all lying right next to each other. If there was no free space in units, they were simply kept in the hallways.

Masks, scrubs, and protective eye shields for personnel were still catastrophically lacking. Hospital police on guard duty would ask us for masks; in all the chaos, they weren't included in the list of employees eligible for personal protective equipment. Many police officers now looked tired and indifferent, just like the rest of us. Some of them became sick with COVID during their shift and were taken to the ER as patients. It was an odd picture: a uniformed police officer lying on a bed being pushed down a hallway by a nurse.

The lobby was now always crowded with paramedics constantly delivering new patients. On the flip side, it was obvious that day by day, each shift contained fewer nurses, doctors, and clerks. The same personnel were working double shifts. Strewn around the floor of the department were tubes from drips, dirty gowns, and bloodstained sheets. There were not enough custodians.

Dr. Harris and Dr. Mercy both worked not just as administrators, but on active-duty shifts, like ordinary doctors, replacing sick colleagues.

The ER quickly turned into a nursing home before our eyes. Old men and women—many with dementia, in oxygen masks, on drips, or connected to machines—lay on beds and looked ahead with eyes that comprehended nothing. They tore off their masks or disconnected their drips. Relatives were not allowed to visit them. Some of them were brought to the ER from nursing homes in such a state that they had only a few hours to live. They were grayish in color and virtually unconscious. Looking at yet another such old man or woman, I angrily thought, wasn't this person's condition noticed in the nursing home?! How were they allowed to get to this state — to be at death's door before being taken to the ER?! I concluded that many of these old people died not from illness, as such, but from the lack of proper care for them during illness.

Near the ER, just by the back of the exterior door and not far from my windows, three mobile morgues were recently parked: three shiny, sun-reflecting, long metallic vans on wheels. Inside, the coolers were on, and the engines of all three vans rumbled in unison — *rrrrr*.

* * *

What did I do in the ER now? Hell, nothing much. I helped doctors save drug addicts who were overdosing (by the way, it was catastrophic spike of drug overdose at this time.) Because of the significant shortage of staff, I helped police officers to restrain and calm psych patients; staff who cared for the demented elderly, helping feed them. A few times I helped workers from Mortuary Division move dead bodies from the hospital bed onto the special "red bed" on which corpses are being transported to the morgue. In short, I worked wherever I was needed. One day, my nerves got to me and in the middle of my shift I jumped in my car and drove home. Halfway there, I made a U-turn and went back.

"Do I Love Him?"

After work, I'd bring Amy to my place, and we would often walk in the salt marsh. Due to quarantine, there were almost no other interesting places to take strolls anyway. We didn't want to recall our recent conflict and her epileptic seizure.

We walked a lot through the marsh, discovering its remote, unexplored corners, meadows, and thicket-covered paths, and watched the tides go in and out. We debated and discussed various topics, such as art, politics, and everything else under the sun. We talked about the pandemic finally coming to an end but leaving a huge mark for the suffering it's caused. A lot should change for the better, not just the exposed inefficiency of the country's health care system. People will change self-consciousness and their way of life. They will draw the right conclusions. And they won't create new weapons—conventional or of mass destruction—atomic or biological. No more wars! We'll stop depleting natural resources and destroying the environment. The endless, insatiable pursuit of success, wealth, and power will also end. A completely different existence will take over the globe…

* * *

One day we were driving up to her house, when she suggested we pay a visit to some fishermen nearby. One of her neighbors was among them and had been inviting Amy for a while with the promise of a great catch.

"Why don't we go there now?" she suggested.

We drove up to a small vacant lot on the shore of the bay, where we saw about a dozen fishermen. They had turned the place into a kind of chill zone. Here they not only fished but also roasted marshmallows and hot dogs on the grill, smoked weed, drank beer and vodka, and discussed what was going on in their projects.

Our appearance at first met with wary looks. But when Amy greeted her neighbor, he explained to his friends that this was his "beautiful neighbor" and her boyfriend. After that we were like one of their own. They treated us to hot dogs and even passed us joints. Amy immediately found herself in the spotlight, listening to their adventures and anecdotes and exploding with laughter. Here, among these rough fishermen from the projects, she felt natural and comfortable, just as she had at the Cotton Club while amongst musicians and jazz fans. That was my impression, anyway; I don't know how comfortable she really was.

We were about to leave, when one of the fishermen hooked some big fish and, either jokingly or seriously, asked Amy if she wanted to reel it in. She jumped at the chance. The fish was really resisting, and Amy soon got tired trying to land it. She asked me to help her. We took turns, our strength gradually diminishing, but the fish persisted, not wanting to give up. The fishermen gathered around us in a semicircle, cheerfully shouting and encouraging us while drinking beer, and with a net at the ready. Finally, in a joint effort, we pulled a large sand shark out of the water. It jumped on the grass, where metal bottle tops and cigarette butts were scattered about.

Amy, being indescribably overjoyed at all this, wanted to take the shark off the hook. But it wasn't easy—the shark squirmed and twisted with all its might, threatening to bite.

"Aah!" Amy suddenly screamed, raising her hand sharply and recoiling. She brought her palm close to her, fingers outstretched.

Standing nearby I could see a thin stream of blood slowly flowing down her palm. It was clear what had happened: inexperienced, Amy made a wrong move, and the shark bit her finger with its sharp teeth. Apparently, the cut wasn't deep. I wanted to approach her, but suddenly…

"Kee-eeeee-arr!" A strange cry rang out, and a falcon, lightning fast, came down from somewhere above like a stone falling from the sky. He sank his claws into the shark and began to peck at it with his hooked beak. The shark struggled to avoid the attack, wriggling and trying to sweep the bird off with its tail, but the bird had an obvious advantage. Still, the falcon almost got hit. It would scamper away but stay close, then rush to attack again with indignant, menacing cries. Its beak dug into the shark's body, leaving torn, bloody wounds on its back and belly. He pecked out the shark's eyes and ripped out the intestines from its torn belly. Feathers flew in the air.

It was an eerie, gripping scene. We all stood amazed. Some fishermen pointed their cell phones at the two beautiful and mysterious predators, filming without a word. Even for seasoned fishermen, this bloody bout was extraordinary.

After a while, the shark lay lifeless on the ground. The falcon, uttering a wrathful cry, flew off. He was evidently battered, flying low and slow as if he would fall out of the sky at any given moment.

We were all standing in shock at what we had seen.

"It's a message from God, Ben! That's what's waiting for us!" Amy suddenly exclaimed and made the sign of the cross. Her whole body shook. "I don't want to be here any longer. Let's get out of here."

* * *

The long branches of a tree almost reached the windows of the apartment. Now, at night, the shadows cast by these branches moved along the ceiling and along the walls of the room. Throwing her hands behind her head on the soft pillow, Amy watched this amusing show and pretended she was in some magical forest.

"Jason is getting released soon," she said to herself. "He wrote to me that, due to COVID, they're giving early release to those prisoners whose sentences are almost up and who behaved well in prison. They started getting COVID cases there too. And deaths. Especially Blacks, whom he says make up the vast majority in their prison. Racism is still everywhere. Jason writes that he misses me a lot. He says he's now going to live right and make only legit money. He will return to the fitness club and do what he did before, coach athletes. He's a man of his word.

"To be honest, it was I who dragged him into the whole pill fiasco. I had just graduated from nursing school then. I had gotten a job as a nurse, and our romantic love was at its peak. I became possessed with a lust for pleasure. We moved into a nice apartment and bought a new car. Money was already scarce, and debt was growing, but I wanted to go on a cruise around the world. That's when I came up with the crazy idea about the pills. As a result, our round-the-world journey ended on the dock. But now Jason says he's going to make a U-turn. God, how I want him to come back now, today, and take me right away with him! Because if not, it may be too late, and I will not want to return to him."

The wall clock ticked amid silence.

Turning to her right side, Amy looked at the profile of Ben's face, who was sleeping next to her. Carefully, so as not to wake him up, she lightly touched the bridge of his nose with her index finger and ran it along its length. Her eyes were used to the darkness, and she could clearly see how Ben slightly twitched his nostrils, snoring as if he were going to sneeze, and then turned on his side with his back to her. "Ben is cool, smart dude. Things are interesting with him. He loves me madly. He is being more insistent on me moving in with him. Maybe I really should move in and stay with him. Yeah, he's White and therefore didn't even realize he's still a racist. Do I love him?"

She was hoping to finally get an answer to the question that she'd been asking herself more and more often lately—*Why am I constantly asking myself this now? Why does this bother me so much? Do I love him? Do I? Or am I just playing the game of love with him?*

For some reason, she recalled the deadly fight between the shark and the falcon that they witnessed this morning on the shore. It sent chills down her spine. She made the sign of the cross.

Letting Loose

The noisy, restless city that never sleeps was overtaken by the incessant howl of EMS sirens and was plunging into some kind of dark lethargic state. We are going to reach a so-called "plateau".

When I'd go to the ER every day and change my clothes, I felt in my gut that the situation had continued to worsen — even though it seemed that it couldn't get any worse — and that we were sinking into some kind of hellish bottom.

Both secretaries at our front desk were ill. In the next room, the ER's head nurse was sick as well. Dr. Mercy lay in the critical ward at a special veterans' hospital in New Jersey. He had developed bilateral pneumonia and was on a ventilator. I heard from Dr. Harris that "Adam will fight through hell to survive."

Until just recently, I was sharing a small office with Dr. Mercy. We sat next to each other, without wearing masks, coughing and sneezing, and now he was sick with COVID. Now I sat in the office alone. I didn't understand why I hadn't gotten infected yet.

* * *

The Black giant psych technician Steven was now changing into scrubs in the mornings in my office, where I sat alone now. Before taking off his clothes, Steven would open a new scrub to make sure he was given the right size. A special size was ordered for him, larger than even XXL. He'd lift a giant blue jacket and pants in front of him and, nodding approvingly that the size was correct, take off his sweater, exposing his mighty, tattooed body.

"Ben, I used to work as a prison guard. I saw riots and unrest. I worked with the rescue team during Sandy. But none of that is even close to what is happening now. Here in the ER, I'm often asked to help place the dead on a "red bed" to transport them to the morgue. You know when a person dies, he quickly becomes cold and heavy. And most of them had COVID. It's not my job, but I'm asked because Mortuary is short of staff, and I give them a hand. We're all short of staff here, short of medicine, we only have a lot of sick and dead. Ye-eh, man…" He looked out the tiny window under the ceiling, in which a piece of the sky was visible. "I have a large family—five children and elderly parents. I have no right to go down; I have to hold on."

"I understand, Steve. We all have to hold on. Give me a high-five."

* * *

"Ben! Ben! Are you here?" Dr. Harris called me from his office.

"Yes, doc."

"How's it going?"

I didn't answer.

"Ben, are you fucking deaf? Come here."

"What's up, doc?" I entered the boss's office.

He sat at his desk with his hand pressed against his fleshy cheek. His face looked kind of strange. I had not seen him like this until now—his eyes madly fluttered about, his lips twisted, and the nostrils of his small, straight nose twitched. Wheezing, he pierced me with the gaze of his angry and, at the same time, unhappy eyes.

"Ben, you're good with alcoholics, right?"

"Yeah, I understand something about their mentality."

"So, you can determine whether someone has the mentality of an alcoholic?"

"Hmm." I did not understand what he was getting at.

"If, for example, I now want to drink a liter of vodka, then in your opinion, I'm an alcoholic?"

"If you want to drink a liter of vodka for no reason, then for sure you are a full-blown alcoholic," I confirmed, finally noticing that there were playful sparks emanating from his eyes. I realized that Dr. Harris was just messing with me now.

"Do you really want to get drunk, doc?" I asked directly.

"Yeah."

"All the restaurants and bars are closed. But we can get drunk at my house, especially since we live practically next door to each other."

* * *

We were sitting in the living room of my apartment—Dr. Harris, Amy, and me. Dr. Harris and I drank Absolut vodka and Amy drank orange juice, explaining that "vodka is not my drink of choice, even if I wanted to drink, but there's no wine at home."

We bought a liter, just in case. I was sure that the two of us would be able to drink half a bottle at most. To my surprise and contrary to my expectations, we'd already drunk three-quarters. Despite this, we weren't drunk, but rather fully relaxed.

Dr. Harris either reminisced about his student years or told curious, slightly dirty stories from his surgery practice. At first, he wasn't sure if Amy would be offended by them, but seeing how she liked it, he let loose and told his medical anecdotes without hesitation, sometimes throwing in foul language or gesticulating wildly. He abruptly fell silent near the end of one of his stories, looked carefully at Amy and me, pursed his lips, and then gave away the surprise ending: "…and she has potatoes in her vagina! A potato this big! It turns out someone told her you can prevent the prolapse of the uterus with them!"

We all exploded with laughter.

On the table there were saucers with olives, cubes of cheese, and sliced pieces of grilled chicken.

Then Dr. Harris told Amy how we met on the salt marsh when we were fishing on the shore.

"Ben caught a sand shark this big!" He spread his arms to show the length of the shark. "No joke — it almost bit off his finger!"

He was exaggerating, of course, but it was still a really cool, big shark!

"He dragged it with such stubbornness and determination that I decided right then and there that this guy should work for me in the ER."

"I also recently caught a big shark. It took a bite of my finger," she stuck out her finger with a fresh narrow scar on it.

"No joke," Dr. Harris said after glancing at the scar.

He and I continued to drink vodka like it was water. We didn't realize how much stress was on us and how tired we were. I'm talking about myself; I can't imagine the stress Dr. Harris was under.

"So, you're that same nurse Ben wanted us to hire in the ER?" he asked, putting an empty glass on the table.

"Yes," Amy replied.

"Well, remind me about what happened and why you weren't hired," he asked.

Amy was embarrassed for a moment, but quickly getting up the nerve and pulling herself together, she said: "I worked at a medical center…and, as a nurse, had easy access to pills. I was living with my boyfriend at the time…" Here she fell silent. She was ashamed to continue.

"Aaaah, it's clear. Now I remember—because of pill's story, you got a couple of years' probation, and your nursing license was suspended, right?"

"Yep. It is what it is."

"But now, after everything that's happened, you realize the mistake you made, right?" he asked.

"Yes," she nodded.

Dr. Harris wrinkled his forehead, thinking about something. "Do you still want to work at the ER? Even now, with this fucking COVID and no one knowing how it's all going to end?"

"Yes."

"Ben, do you think we should fight for her and take her on? So, the girl took a wrong turn—it can happen to anyone. We need to give her a chance and help her. Ok, I'll talk to HR about you. I think we can figure it out and find a suitable job for you in the ER.”

“Doctor, are you serious? No joke?” Amy asked, in a mocking manner imitating Dr. Harris's favorite phrase.

“Absolutely.” He answered firmly, pouring more vodka from the bottle. He was still hopelessly trying to get hammered.

* * *

It was around midnight when Amy and I escorted Dr. Harris to his car. Amy offered to drive him home, since she was the only one of us who was sober, but he refused since he was a stone's throw from his house.

Soon we were back home. Amy started to clean the table. She put the dishes in the dishwasher, and I sat on the sofa. My head was spinning faster. Only now did I realize that I was completely plastered.

“Your boss has very beautiful, muscular arms; I couldn't take my eyes off them. They reminded me of the arms of ancient heroes carved in marble statues.”

“He doesn't just have the arms of a hero; he's the very definition of a hero. A few days ago, he covered half of the ER by himself because the other doctors who were supposed to work that shift were sick. You're a nurse; can you imagine—one doctor for fifty patients, most in critical condition? He's not the only one. In the ER, we have giant Steven, a technician-overseer. He also falls under the category of hero as well as several other doctors and nurses. In real life, baby, true heroes aren't at all what we imagine them to be. Heroes are simple: they laugh, curse, and tell dirty stories about prolapses of the uterus. They're not looking for attention. But they have one rare quality: risking their health and their lives for the sake of others, not even thinking that they themselves are heroes."

I remained silent for a short while. "I don't know if my dad ever told you that his dad, my grandpa, escaped from a Nazi concentration camp. So, after the war, he moved to the U. S. The press wrote about him, and he got invitations to do radio and TV appearances. I didn't know him when he was alive, but those relatives who did told me that in everyday life he was the most ordinary person. He liked to tell dirty jokes. On the outside, there was nothing heroic about him. By the way, I was named after him."

"So, you're also a hero," Amy said, sitting down next to me and putting her hand on my shoulder. "Do you think your boss will be able to get me into the ER?"

"Of course—consider it already done. You see, it didn't work out for you the first time, but it will now. Soon we'll work together, you'll also move in with me, and everything finally becomes great," I stroked Amy's black, rough hair.

"Yeah," she agreed and looked at me with incomprehensible sadness.

"Hey, what's wrong? You don't look like you're happy." I leaned back and squinted with one eye to see Amy better. I felt very dizzy already and everything around me was somehow blurry.

"No, I'm happy, very happy. Amen!" she concluded, standing up. "Come on, my alcoholic, I'll help you get to bed. Hopefully tomorrow morning you'll be able to get up and go to work. Wait—I forgot that tomorrow is Saturday and you're off! Or are you going to work tomorrow?"

"Tomorrow is Saturday and I'm off, and as a real Jew, I observe Shabbat. I'm gonna go to the synagogue tomorrow. Shema, Yisrael! I wanna pray. Yes, I wanna pray and tell God that He hasn't got even a drop of mercy for humans. He sees this entire fucking Armageddon, our suffering and death, and doesn't give a shit. Yes, He doesn't give a shit!" I repeated as we walked into the bedroom with her supporting me under my arm.

"Okay, okay. You may tell God all you want. Just be careful first; don't fall."

After a couple of minutes, I was lying on the bed with my face buried in the pillow, and Amy was pulling off my socks and jeans.

Hero and Savage

I opened my eyes and pulled on my ear to ensure I wasn't still sleeping, and it wasn't a dream. Amy seemed to be floating toward me in a light-colored, thin robe. She carefully carried a tray bearing a steaming hot cup of coffee, shiny granules of sugar, and a glass of milk.

"Good morning, my dear. Happy Shabbat!" She put the tray on the nightstand. "Do you have a hangover after yesterday? Do you need Tylenol?"

"Thanks, I'm fine." I lied.

"Then drink your favorite coffee. Add the milk and sugar yourself."

"I feel like I'm in seventh heaven! Coffee in bed!"

"I have to pay tribute to my hero in some way."

"Stop with the bullshit hero talk," I muttered, sitting up against the headboard. I poured the milk into my coffee, threw in the sugar, and began stirring the mix with my spoon.

Amy sat down next to me. She looked at me and said haltingly, "I want to ask you a huge favor."

"What favor?"

"Just swear you will not get offended. Feel free to say no."

"Shoot."

"Could you…could you lend me some money? You know, I need to pay off my lawyer. He's on my ass about it. I'm terribly uncomfortable asking you for money…I'm very ashamed." She grimaced.

"How much do you need?"

"How much? At least five thousand. But ten would be even better."

"Wow! I'm not sure. I need to think about it."

It wasn't just the amount Amy asked for that confused me. It seemed suspicious and strange to me that she suddenly needed so much money. Moreover, until now, she had never mentioned a lawyer who was supposedly "on her ass."

"Benji, dear, I really, really need this money," she put her hand on my chest and began to gently stroke, knowing how this gesture makes me feel so excited. "You can't even imagine how I'm suffering because of this debt." Tears shone in her eyes.

I started to feel sorry for her. After a moment's hesitation, I put down my cup of unfinished coffee. I took her palm, brought it to my lips, and kissed it.

"Fine."

"What? You're willing to lend me ten thousand bucks???"

"Yes. When do you need it by?"

"As soon as possible. Preferably now."

"Do you have Zelle?"

She nodded.

Without saying any more words, I picked up my cell phone.

"You can't imagine how much you're helping me out, Benji," she repeated staring at the cell phone in my hands.

I started to input all the information into my phone to complete the transaction. Amy closed her eyes and appeared to be praying.

A few minutes passed. Finally, in the silence, the click of her cell phone sounded, indicating that a new message was received.

"Oh my God!" She screamed after seeing a notification on her cell phone that the money had been transferred to her account. She bent down, wrapped her hands around my face and kissed me a few times. "Benji, my love! You're not just a hero, you're a saint! I'll give everything back down to the last penny, you'll see."

I wrapped my arms around her waist, trying to draw her in close. But she freed herself, got up, and flew out of the room.

Soon I could hear the sound of the shower from the bathroom. I waited for her to come back, freeing some room next to me on the bed.

Indeed, after her shower she did return to the bedroom. But to my surprise, she wasn't naked or in her robe as I had expected, but rather in a skirt and bra, buttoning her blouse as she walked in.

"Are you leaving?" I asked out of surprise. "Why? I thought we'd spend the whole day together."

"No, I can't. Unfortunately, I've got a bunch of urgent errands to run. I should go."

"What? Hold on. What a bunch of urgent arrands?" I quickly got up and blocked her way out of the room by standing in the doorway with my hands pressed against the doorframe on both sides. You're not going anywhere. I need to know the answer here and now."

"Don't act like a fool! I'll explain everything to you to-morrow. C'mon!"

"Tell me the truth, where are you going right now? Tell me the truth! What do you need the money for?"

"It's none of your fucking business! Let me go!" She shouted so that her neck tensed up.

What made me so angry wasn't that I had just given her the money so recklessly, but that I felt cheated. It was obvious that she was hiding the truth from me.

And it suddenly became clear to me that we were going to break up now! That thought struck me like a flash of lightning.

I knelt in front of her, wrapping my arms around her legs.

"Stay with me! I don't want you to leave!"

"Stop this drama. Hey, hey—what are you doing?! Aah!"

As tightly as I could, I pressed her hips against me, then rose from my knees and lifted her clear off the floor. As I threw her over my shoulder, she started pounding my back.

"Bastard! Reptile!"

But I carried her to the bed, feeling like the ancient Roman in the well-known sculpture *Ratto delle Sabine.*

After some time, we were lying next to each other. There were signs of a recent struggle in the room: the cloth, blanket, and pillows were scattered on the floor, the sheet on the bed was crumpled.

"I want to tell you, Benji, you're not just a hero and a saint, you're also a fucking savage." She paused and continued, "Not long ago you swore you would never hurt me again. And you have already forgotten. You have no idea how much pain you've caused me right now. And they say it's only Black men who rape White women. Well, now I can leave you with peace of mind."

She got up, dressed slowly, not even looking in my direction. And she left without saying goodbye.

Like a Bird in a Cage

The next morning, Amy walked along the platform at Grand Central Station, wearing a long, loose, pink knit dress with an unbuttoned short denim jacket over it and leather sandals on her feet. She occasionally glanced at her new silver watch and then at a large electronic schedule board on the wall, where information about arriving trains was updated. It stated that the train from upstate, which she was waiting for, was due to arrive on time, in ten minutes.

Amy rolled her eyes up to the high ceiling of the station, drew in a deep breath, and cringed her face. She felt sorry for herself.

"My man! Jason! I can't believe my eyes! Finally!"

"Yeeee!" She was swept up in a hug by a thin Black man of about 35, in a white T-shirt and jeans who just gotten off the train.

"I don't believe this is real and not a dream." Amy whispered, closing her eyes and exposing her face and neck to his kisses.

"My love, my queen! I don't know how I was able to live without you these two years." Jason showered her with kisses, pressing her tightly to him. Then he distanced himself from her, as if wanting to make sure that this was not a dream, and that Amy was really in his arms.

The few passengers who got off the arriving train quickly dispersed, and only Amy and Jason remained on the long, empty platform.

Amy stroked his cheeks and got up on tip toes to kiss him on the lips.

"I was like a bird in a cage without you for two years. God, how happy I am!"

She kissed him again and they headed for the exit. Jason carried a backpack thrown over one shoulder, wrapping his other arm around Amy. Her arm was also wrapped around his waist. He was telling her how this morning when he bought a ticket to New York, he nearly got on the wrong train and almost ended up in Pennsylvania. Amy heartily laughed.

From the outside, it seemed that in the entire city of many millions there was no happier couple.

Saint Mary Magdalene

The next day, Amy and Ben's father were returning home after grocery shopping. Mark was behind the wheel of his Grand Cherokee with Amy in the passenger seat.

"Mark, stop here," Amy said.

"Here?"

"Yes, near the church, please. I want to go in there."

He stopped the car near St. Mary's Church, with a cross topping its high dome.

"Thank you. I won't be long."

She got out of the car and, climbing the steps, disappeared behind the high doors of the church.

There wasn't a single soul inside. Several candles were burning in front of the statues of the saints, and on either side of the altar were two large baskets with white flowers. Sunlight streamed through the multicolored stained-glass windows, making it seem that angels, chariots, saints, and prophets were in continuous movement. In different locations there were tables with bottles of sanitizer and signs reminding parishioners to wear masks inside the sanctuary.

Inhaling the scents of flowers and wax, Amy slowly walked toward the altar. She crossed herself, silently said a prayer and, turning her gaze to the Crucifixion, dropped to her knees on the marble steps in front of the altar.

After a while, she stood up and went to the table, where there were various brochures with prayers, and appeals to parishioners for donations. She took a clean sheet of paper and a pencil from the table, and after briefly fixing her narrowed eyes on the high dome, began to write something.

When she had finished writing, she took an envelope from the table, folded the paper she had written on in thirds, and put it in the envelope. Then she headed for the exit, where Mark was waiting for her in the car.

"Sorry for making you wait so long," she apologized, as she sat on the seat.

"No worries, it's okay."

"Mark, could you give this to Ben?" She handed him the sealed envelope.

He took the envelope and inspected it in his hands.

"Such a romantic gesture, like one of those old-fashioned love stories. Okay, I'll give it to him. So, ready to go?"

"Yes. I'll help you bring in the bags and then I'll leave," she said.

He didn't say anything. They drove a few blocks, leaving the noisy street behind, and turned onto a tree-lined road where there were few cars.

"After your prayer in the church, you probably feel like Saint Mary Magdalene, right?" Mark asked her with some slight irony.

Lately, something had clearly changed in their relationship. When he would talk to her, there was often irony and sarcasm in his voice.

"Yes, almost." Amy reacted coldly to his joke. "I don't know if I should tell you about it or not, but I have long wanted to confess to you that you remind me of my stepfather in some way. My stepfather was not partial toward me. Simply put, he wanted to fuck me since I had been a teenager. But he didn't dare to. So, to compensate for it, he treated me very badly. I have the impression that you have similar issues toward me."

"You're wrong; it's all in your fantasies."

"Mark, why do you despise me so much? Is it because I'm Black?" she asked directly.

Mark chuckled.

"No, honey. It's because of who you are in general. I've studied you during the time we've spent together. I'm really pissed at you—mad at the fact that you hypnotized my son and messed him up to the point where he's completely lost his mind. If you stay with Ben, you'll make him a beggar. I know what I'm talking about. You're one of those women who doesn't know how to earn money but knows how to spend it on all sorts of nonsense. God only knows what. Unfortunately, Ben is a loco. He doesn't see the obvious, and I can't influence him in any way." He patted himself with his free hand on the thigh, where not so long ago he always kept a pack of cigarettes in his jeans pocket. "Fuck, I forget every time that I quit smoking."

"Mark, I hate listening to you. Do you know why? Because you have no idea who I actually am. Unlike you, I don't base my love off of money. For me love is not money, but a matter of life or death. I thought you were smarter than you really are. Well, then consider yourself lucky, you're getting your wish. I left Ben. And today is my last day with you. Please, stop the car and let me out."

The brakes squealed and the car skidded to a stop, leaving wide black stripes from the tires on the asphalt. If

Amy didn't have her seatbelt on, she probably would have banged her head against the windshield.

"Now listen to me carefully, Holy Magdalene. Please, make sure that I never see you in my life again. Stay in your shitty ghetto and forget about Ben. Got it?" He bent over her seat, reached over to the metal handle with his hand, and opened the door. "Get out, dirty whore!"

Amy sat silently for a moment as if contemplating an adequate response. Unexpectedly, she answered him calmly. "You're right, absolutely right. I'm a dirty whore, and you're an old fool," and left the car.

Truth or Dare

"**M**y dear Ben,
I want to let you know that Jason returned. Due to the pandemic, they released him early. He's been living with me for the last few days. I should have told you about it earlier, before he came back. Sorry.

But I'll not stay with Jason either.

I'm leaving New York to write my novel. No more excuses. I have to make it or break. Period.

How long will I be gone for? Maybe a few months, maybe for half a year or even more. I can't say for sure.

Will I come back to you? Or to Jason? I don't know this yet. For a long time, I was sure that Jason was the man for me, and I'd spend eternity with him. But since I've been with you, everything's changed.

Now I've come to the only right decision, which is to leave New York. I have to leave, work on my novel, and figure myself out.

Thank you for the money you lent me. I lied to you about the lawyer. I needed that money to leave. I'll refund it to you as soon as I can.

In any case, it's fair to let you know so you won't wait for me. You're free to fly. Goodbye, Ben—goodbye and forgive me."

After reading the letter, I carefully folded it and put it back into the envelope. Then I turned to the window. Was it really true? I thought she left me that damned morning because of my savage behavior. But, as it turned out now, the whole business was not about me, or rather, not only about me. My premonition that I would soon part with her, that she was going to leave me, did not deceive me.

"Did she go back to that convict?" my dad asked.

All this time, he was sitting in his recliner, watching baseball. Now he stood up and walked up behind me.

"Did she or not?" he repeated.

I turned to face him. "She didn't go back to him, but she did dump me, and she's left New York."

"Very good. Thank God."

* * *

Soon I was driving through the streets of the familiar ghetto. It was early evening; the road construction crews were finished for the day. My car bounced on potholes and shallow pits as it looped and detoured to get to the right street. Finally, I stopped in front of the old four-story house where Amy lived.

Getting out of the car, I looked longingly at her window on the second floor. It was closed, and the light was not on in the room, but it was still too bright for that anyway.

Wrinkling my forehead, I looked at that window, hoping her intuition would whisper that I was there. But that didn't happen.

I called her several times on the phone as I sat there, but the electronic voice monotonously replied, "This voicemail has not been set up yet." Then I went to McDonald's, bought coffee and French fries, and came back again. The lights in her apartment were still not on. After finishing my healthy meal, I tossed the empty containers on the sidewalk with the rest of the garbage lying around, wiped my palms, and went up to the second floor. Leaning my ear against the door, I strained to catch at least some sound coming from behind it but didn't hear a thing.

I went back down and sat in the car again, peering at everyone who came in and out of that house. Finally, I noticed a tall, athletic-looking man in his mid-thirties, wearing a white baseball cap, black glasses, wide jeans, and a loose black T-shirt. It's him! Jason! I immediately remembered the man in the photo on Amy's dresser.

He walked through the entrance door, and a few minutes later a light came on in the window of Amy's apartment.

Minutes after this, I was again at her door. I pressed the doorbell before pulling the mask up higher on my face. The door opened.

"Hello," I said.

"Hi." The man I recognized on the street answered, sizing me up suspiciously.

"Amy lives here, right?"

"Yes."

"Can I talk to her?"

"She's not home right now," he replied, remaining wary. "Bro, who are you?"

"I'm her probation officer." I took my hospital ID out of my jeans pocket and just as quickly shoved it back in. "She missed the appointment I made, and her phone doesn't answer. Do you know when she's going to be home?"

"No, I don't," he replied. My appearance as a supposed probation officer and the way that I presented my plastic ID was probably not entirely convincing to him, but as a man released from prison just a few days ago, he didn't want to make even any possible waves with representatives of the law.

"In that case, please tell her that I came by and ask her to call me back."

"Okay, what's your name?"

"Ben. Mister Ben. She knows my telephone number."

PART FIVE

The Aftermath

We slowly descended from the "plateau." Workers who had been sick with COVID were slowly returning to the ER. The familiar faces of those who hadn't been around for a while were back. Doctors, nurses, hospital police, and maintenance workers resumed their roles. Buses with medical staff from other states finally arrived for support.

Every day now I was dressed in new scrubs. I wore a transparent plastic protective shield over my eyes and an N-95 face mask. The shield quickly got covered with sweat, the tight elastic bands of the hard mask cut into my face and ears after wearing it for a long time, and my skin itched from the scrubs worn over my naked body. All in the name of protection.

In the office across from me, Dr. Mercy sat at his desk like before. He had not completely recovered yet after recently suffering severe bilateral pneumonia. His face was still pale, with some unhealthy pinkish spots. He was all hunched over and had lost weight—at least twenty pounds—but his weight loss didn't contribute to a healthy appearance. He looked tired, about ten years older than he was.

Fairly recently, as an assistant director, he had walked through the ER hallways handing out orders and instructions to staff. I remember when I compared him to God then, who sent arriving souls in different directions depending on what each deserved. Now Dr. Mercy gave the impression of a man who himself had spent some time on the other side, where he was being tortured by demons and then sent back to us, to this sinful land.

One day while sitting in the office, Dr. Mercy told me about the month-long battle with his illness in the veteran's hospital. A few times he thought that it was the end, he would not survive, but still managed to get strength from somewhere.

"My daughter still needs me. I can't leave her before getting her on her feet." He smiled, but as though he was going to cry.

Dr. Mercy smiled in different ways. Sometimes it was sharp, rigid, and mechanical stretching his fleshy cheeks and thick lips. This was when he was preparing to reprimand someone from the staff. It reflected his tough nature as a former military man. But he also had another smile—charming, light, with a hint of sadness. It revealed the other side of his delicate, maybe even very vulnerable soul.

"Doc, you have so many antibodies now you can sell them! You have nothing to fear; no virus is a match for you anymore," I joked.

"Maybe the virus isn't so deadly anymore for some of us, but it's too early to relax. You don't need to wear a mask but carry a gun. Gun! You see what's happening with law and order now. When I left the army, I kept my gun, and am glad I did. I suggest you do the same, Ben. Just get a piece, like a Beretta or a Glock."

"Doctor, you know better than me how difficult and risky it is to get a gun in New York City. If it's illegal, you risk going to jail. And legal permission will take a hundred years."

"Yes, I know." Dr. Mercy adjusted his glasses and looked at me carefully. "I have a good friend in the sheriff's office. Once I helped him a lot, and now, if I need to, I can always turn to him. So, everything will be done kosherly and without unnecessary red tape."

"Ok, doc, let me think about it."

* * *

Meanwhile, in distant Minneapolis, the murder of George Floyd caused a new wave to roll across the country—this time a wave of racial protests. These protests quickly reached New York, further increasing the degree of social tension that went beyond purely racial problems. The foundations of our social system were teetering from an ever-present unpredictability and uncertainty in everything.

In New York, the tension was omnipresent: in rude and insolent manners, in people shouting over each other in "conversations", in people acting out in irritation from standing in long lines, and in the aggressive manner of drivers on the roads. There seemed to be a continuous, swirling argument over politics, Trump, poor service, high prices—you name it—between relatives, coworkers, acquaintances, and strangers. It was as if everyone was looking for an excuse to get into an argument to vent their maxed-out anger and frustration.

This incivility crept into our beloved Marine Park neighborhood. Near my house, where not so long ago it was always quiet and clean, there was always garbage that no one picked up. Strong storms would sometimes sweep through, downing many trees, but no one bothered to pick them up. Drug users occupied benches in the alleys now, where usually there would be couples in love. In parked cars, more and more windows started to be broken. Eventually, gunshots could be heard at night.

Then a wave of criminality swept across the entire country, including New York, and especially Manhattan, where hundreds of prestigious stores and bank branches were looted by gangs. Brooklyn wasn't spared, either. Not far from my house, Kings Plaza was also destroyed and looted, including dozens of prestigious stores and several supermarkets and car dealerships.

The police remained virtually inactive, fearing accusations of racism or anti-liberalism. Right at this time, the presidential race was in full swing, and political passions were heating up. Just as the Republicans stubbornly "ignored" the significant medical scale of the pandemic, the Democrats did not mention the rampant crime and police inaction. It was obvious that the life of an ordinary person was not worth a red cent to politicians, regardless of their party affiliation.

Everyone who could acquire weapons; having one's own gun was no longer a whim, but a reliable way to protect oneself. I also finally decided that I should take Dr. Mercy's advice to get a piece.

Amy, Amy, Everywhere

Occasionally when I returned from work in the evening, my neighbors—old men and women—would be assembled near the entrance of the building. They were honoring the "heroes of the pandemic," banging on metal plates and cups. It was loud enough to hear on all six floors of the building.

I'd approach the house while still in my light blue hospital scrubs, waving at them in greeting. In response, they delightedly upped the sound, banging even harder. Several times I jokingly asked them to "perform" my favorite tunes by The Doors.

"Ben, you're a hero! You're now a superstar, more popular than Jim Morrison! Ben, where's your girlfriend? Where's Amy? Every hero must have a girlfriend."

"Amy went to Georgia to visit relatives," I lied.

"Then I can be your girlfriend during her absence. I'm still very hot!" one of the old ladies joked.

And so, throwing meaningless words around to the resounding "timpani," I approached the entrance, near which the magnolia bloomed its delicate flowers.

I looked at the familiar white dove that often sat on the tree branch or walked on the thick, green grass, searching for worms and bugs. During that year, since the dove had chosen our courtyard as its habitat, it had noticeably grown and gained strength, turning from a thin birdie into a strong, proud bird. During the day, it flew from one window to another or from the bottom floors to the top ones, sitting either on the windowsills, the air conditioners, or the side of the roof. It claimed the house as its own.

Some neighbors superstitiously believed that God had sent this dove to guard our building. Indeed, not a single tenant had died in our complex during the whole time of the pandemic, though several did become very sick. A few times, I'd seen neighbors making the sign of the cross when passing by the dove.

Sometimes I would pick up the smooth, white feathers it had shed on the grass and brought them home. I carefully stored each new feather together with the others, along with the feather from the falcon on my shelf.

* * *

Amy had disappeared. I called her every day, but her phone was still off. She had also vanished from Facebook and Instagram. Several times I kept watch in my car near her house, but I only saw her boyfriend Jason going in and out. Wherever I went, I looked for Black women, hoping to recognize Amy among them.

She left her slippers, washcloth, a comb, a few bottles of nail polish, and black silk tights in my apartment. Like a true fetishist, I stared at these things for a long time, laying them out on the bed, sorting them out, picking them up, and sitting there with my eyes closed, restoring her image down to the smallest details. I pictured the moments when she used the comb on her hair, covered her nails with the polish, and took off or put on the tights. I mentally recreated a real gallery of Amy, as if it was an exhibition of live paintings or fragments of a film in the cinema, one with a single and unique actress.

I still had Amy's drafts at home. When inspired, she would take a piece of paper and pen and write down some lines, even entire pages. Then I would accidentally find them all over the apartment. It always surprised me that she didn't keep many of them. I preserved them in a special folder as if they were the most valuable documents—bound for future auctions, museums, and libraries. I reread them, and from the frequent repetition of my favorite lines, I even memorized some of them. *"Life is the Word. This Word lives in me. It is conceived in me, deep in my uterus, where it grows and yearns to express itself through me. The Word gradually becomes me and I it…"* Such poetic lines!

Here is another piece about her Black background: *"Sometimes I feel like I carry all the pain of the past with me. It's like I carry all the struggles of Black women who were slaves, who were raped, beaten, and tortured by dogs. These horrors and cruelties have been passed down to us for generations, and any Black woman born in America carries this trauma in her genes. I don't know what to do with this pain; who can I give it to?"* Reading this passage, I wrinkled my face in annoyance and embarrassment, remembering that damned day when I—let's call a spade a spade—raped her.

I grabbed my cell phone every time I heard it ring in the hope it was her; my heart sank when it wasn't. She had resigned from the home attendant agency where she worked, and no one knew anything about her current whereabouts. I don't know how she managed to strike a deal with her probation officer to be able to leave New York—if she even did. She never told me the officer's name, otherwise it might have been a good lead to find her.

It's impossible to imagine that currently, a person can suddenly disappear, as if vanishing into thin air without a trace.

No, I'm lying. I'm lying! Amy herself may have physically disappeared, but she came to me in the form of a stray cat walking in the thick bush of the salt marsh. She flew up and swirled over my head in the form of a falcon and seagull, making anxious, piercing screams. She slithered like a dark yellow snake between the black wet rocks on the shore. I listened to her voice in the wind through the tall grass and the rustle of leaves. I asked the waves, the wind, and the stars about her—the very same stars that her eyes reflected when she looked up into the sky during our walks. No wonder I spent so much time there. Even at night I sat on the cold rocks by the shore, recognizing Amy's voice in the splash of the waves.

Sometimes I took the collected white dove feathers off the shelf and laid them out on a table. Then I decided to collect beautiful feathers of other birds—red-winged black birds, turkeys, and crows. I even came across several light gray/brown-striped feathers peregrine falcons had lost. One day I came up with an idea—to glue these feathers together with wire and wax. I decided to construct a whole new bird with them, hoping, like an ancient magus, that it would return Amy to me.

At that time, I didn't need any politics, booze, or other distractions. I still went to work every day, but I was there only physically. Sometimes I forgot which patient I was visiting and for what purpose. A coworker approached—a doctor or nurse—and I would stop and look at them puzzled, trying to understand what they were asking and needed from me.

Delusion

Something odd started happening with my father. He has recovered from his last heart surgery, and everything seemed to have been heading in the right direction. Amy left, another home aide service he refused, believing he would be able to take care of himself.

I must say that my dad belongs to the group of people who are sociable but lonely. These types of people are hardly recognizable. Such a person gives the impression of being friendly and very affable, and easily gets along with people at first glance. But if you observe more closely, you'll see that he doesn't have deep, warm relations with anyone, even with those related to him. All of his sociability and relationships are superficial and deceptive. Why is that? Probably because his primary interest is just himself and no one else; his own concerns take priority. Such people have clear boundaries for their attachments, and this line is rarely crossed.

My mother, God rest her soul, was his complete opposite. She often went above and beyond and had other people's best interests at heart. Because of this, she was valued by relatives, friends, and neighbors alike—by everyone who knew her. I still don't understand how these two completely different people could have gotten together and married. What did they have in common?

Knowing my father's penchant for constantly moving around Brooklyn and his habit of endless shopping, in which he found pleasure incomprehensible to me, my concern from the very start of the pandemic was that he would catch COVID. But now, due to the lockdown, everything had changed and emptied: even in the park near his house, the chess players and gamblers, with whom he sometimes fraternized, had disappeared.

Despite my expectation, my father himself was not very eager to get out, fearing infection. Moreover, he began to take not simple but super-precautionary measures. Something in him changed, especially after Amy left, and most of the time he was alone. Now he often and for long lengths of time remained pensive, became fearful, and seldom spoke. He sat at home, staring at the TV from morning to night, watching baseball or old Hollywood movies without the emotion he had before, and he rarely called me or any of his relatives with whom he had maintained contact. When he would talk to me, it was only about how many COVID patients we had, how many of them were dying, and how old they were.

* * *

During the night, a phone call awakened me. Caller ID showed "Police Precinct #68."

"Hello, can I talk to Mr. Ben Horowitz?" an unfamiliar male voice asked.

"Yes, that's me," I replied, half asleep.

"This is Officer Clark of the 68th Precinct. Sorry to bother you at such a late hour."

"I'm listening." Turning on the desk lamp, I involuntarily shifted my gaze to the wall clock, which showed 2:35 AM.

"Is Mark Horowitz your father?"

"Yeah. Did something happen to him?"

"We don't quite know yet. Your father has disappeared. The door to his apartment is open, but he's not there. A neighbor brought it to our attention. He probably went out somewhere but forgot to close the door behind him. The neighbor checked several times, but since your father never showed up, they called the police. Do you happen to know where he is by any chance? Is he with you?"

"No, and I don't know where he could be," I replied, finally waking up and starting to sort through the various options in my mind about what could have happened to him and where he might be. But nothing that had any credibility came to mind.

"Your father left his cell phone at home. We checked the recordings of his calls today, and only one conversation with you was recorded. He didn't tell you anything about getting ready to go somewhere or stay with someone for the night?"

"No, I don't recall anything like that."

"How is his mental state? Is he mentally healthy? Does he have dementia?"

"He doesn't have dementia," I replied, wondering whether that was really the case.

"Well, then, we'll look for him. We're going to need your help. Where do you live?"

"In Marine Park."

"Could you come down here now? Do you drive?"

"Yes, of course."

I headed down the highway to Bay Ridge. What happened to him? Where did he disappear to, God damn it?!

Parking the car near his house, next to the police car, I put on a mask, went up to the third floor, and entered my father's apartment.

"Mr. Horowitz? Thank you for coming so quickly," the policeman said as he turned to face me. Another cop, also wearing a mask, stood with his backside against the windowsill with arms crossed over his chest. "Let's not waste our time. Did your father ever tell you or any of his friends that he didn't want to live?"

"It's out of the question. And I say this as a professional psychotherapist working in an ER."

"What kind of relationship do you have with him?" The cop continued to inquire, looking at me point-blank. Our conversation seemed to have transformed into an interrogation. "Did he complain about you to anyone? Did he blame you for anything?"

"Our relationship isn't the best, but there's no great animosity if that's what you're referring to."

Our talk was interrupted by the occasional beeps of police radios, and then someone's crackling voice in the speakers.

"Does he drive a car?" the cop continued.

"Yes."

"Where does he usually park it?"

"In the garage, here, in this house."

"Let's go check."

The three of us went down the stairs and entered a large, dimly lit garage.

"Here it is." I pointed to his Grand Cherokee.

One of the cops looked inside and tried to open the car doors, but they were locked.

"Okay, Mr. Horowitz. Show us his latest photos to know what he looks like and tell us what he may have been wearing when he left the house. We'll look for him until tomorrow night, and if we don't find him, we'll report him as a missing person."

Shortly after, the three of us left the building. The police got into their car and drove away. I walked in the direction of the park, not far from there. I headed down its alley ways leading up to the waterfront, peering not only at the empty chess tables and benches but also at the slopes, lined with bushes and trees, to see whether anyone was lying there. Sometimes here and there you could hear the cry of an awakened bird or the crack of a branch of an old tree swaying in the wind. But the park was completely devoid of people.

When I reached the waterfront, I approached the concrete barrier and bent over to see if anyone was there on the rocks. But they were empty as well. Low waves ran over the dark boulders and crashed with a dull clap, retreating backward. The moonlit path stretched across the water, mysteriously shimmering and shining with golden sparkles.

I stayed for a while, fascinated by this magical view. I thought about the fact that the beauty of Creation sometimes quite unexpectedly opens for us to see, but it happens when we're in a rush or preoccupied with some troubles, and not in good state for aesthetic pleasures.

I went back to the car, deciding to drive around the neighborhood near my father's house in the hope of finding him there. After all, he couldn't get far from home. I drove through the empty streets, staring intently at the rare passersby.

"Dad! Dad!" I screamed, hitting the brakes. I jumped out of the car and rushed over to him.

"Ben? Is that you? How did you find me?" my father asked unperturbed.

He was sitting at the bus stop with his legs crossed. He was wearing jeans and a gray windbreaker over a sweater. Although my appearance had surprised him, he still sat without changing his pose, remaining outwardly calm.

"Dad, why are you here? It's four o'clock in the morning and you're at a bus stop! What are you doing here?"

"Why am I here? Well, I'm just sitting here breathing fresh air," he replied. It was clear he was caught by surprise and didn't know what to say.

"What fresh air? What the fuck are you talking about?"

"I'm waiting for the store to open. I really need to buy some food," he finally replied, nodding in the direction of the City Town supermarket, where he usually bought groceries and small household items.

"You need to buy *this* urgently? Are you serious? You have a fridge full of food."

His strange, silly answers began to make me impatient. Was he trying to make me lose my temper? I snorted with some irritation, and then suddenly my gaze fell on a one-story bank building.

"You're waiting for the bank to open, aren't you?" I asked in a low voice, guessing that I had somehow penetrated his secret with a sixth sense.

My father gave me a pensive and wary look for a while. Then he stroked his thinning hair with his palm.

"Yes," he replied quietly.

After some time, we both entered his apartment. While my father took off his shoes and changed his clothes, I called the police, reciting the case number, and was immediately connected to Officer Clark, whom I already knew. I told him that the missing person was found at a bus stop. I explained that my father apparently had some episode of confusion wherein he mistook the morning for evening and became disoriented, not realizing where he was.

"So, no need to file a missing person report."

"Okay, we'll visit him tomorrow morning to make sure. Take care," the cop said.

My dad, meanwhile, sprayed sanitizer on his hands and vigorously rubbed them together, then sat down on the couch. I walked around the room. I saw a pamphlet of coupons lying on the windowsill. Picking up the pamphlet, I flipped through a few pages. Of course, I was glad that my father was found. But now I was worried about something else—what's wrong with him? Is he in his right mind? And how serious is it?

"Do you want to know why I was looking for you?" I asked, changing my stern tone to an affectionate one. "You left your apartment, forgetting to close the door behind you. Your neighbor noticed this and called the police. They got in touch with me, and then we started looking for you. We were going to file a missing person report. In a few days, your portrait would be hanging on all the poles in Brooklyn."

After hearing this story, my father chuckled.

"Then I would become famous like a Hollywood actor."

"Oh, yeah. And you'll get an Oscar for the best performance of a missing person. Why were you waiting for the bank to open?" I asked in a soft, almost sugary voice.

My father sat there staring ahead of him for a while.

"Don't you understand what's going to happen soon?" he finally asked.

"What?"

"Chaos is about to begin, that's what! Chaos! Then fascists will come to power, no matter what they call themselves—left or right, or patriots. And as always, everything will be the fault of the Jews. This has happened more than once in history. So, we need to be well prepared and always have money on hand. ATMs will soon be empty, don't you understand?"

I didn't take my examining eyes off him.

"This morning I wanted to withdraw twenty thousand dollars from the bank. And I wanted it in small bills, because in times of chaos, no one would take large bills for fear of counterfeiting. Nowadays it's almost impossible to get to the bank because of the long lines—everyone needs cash, I'm not the only smart one—so you need to get there early. I advise you to do the same. Got it?"

I nodded silently, trying to comprehend everything I had just heard.

Meanwhile, my father got up and walked over to me. He squinted at me and cringed as if from the cold. Suddenly, he leaned in so close that I felt him breathing on my face. He took my hand and babbled, "Ben, son, son! I'll confess everything to you. Lately, I've been suffering from severe insomnia. I've been suffocated by nightmares and haunted by somber memories. My long-gone parents have begun to appear to me; I sometimes seem to hear their voices. I think about war and the persecution of Jews. I even think often about God—although you know I don't believe in

God…" He wiped his forehead, upon which small drops of sweat had appeared. "And lately I often feel dizzy, so I try to drive as rarely as possible. I didn't want to tell you this so you wouldn't worry. I didn't want you to think of me as loco…"

I'd never seen him like that—agitated, weak, and desperate. It took a lot of effort to calm him down and put him to bed, giving him sleeping pills. I waited for him to fall asleep and quietly walked out.

I drove down the highway back home, thinking about this situation. I needed some time to get my thoughts together. Why didn't I notice that my father was on the brink of a nervous breakdown? Of course, he's under severe stress, like many old people. They're isolated, afraid of and overcome by a fear of death. But I was sure my dad could manage it on his own. I was wrong. Ugh!

My attention was drawn to a bird hovering high in the sky. It began to rapidly descend, and soon flew almost next to me on my left. It tried to keep up, even though my car was moving at high speed. Every now and then, tearing my glance from the road, I focused on it, trying to figure out what kind of bird it was. Suddenly, the bird flew right up and firmly hit the window with her beak.

"Whoa!!" I opened my eyes, pulled on the wheel, and slammed on the brakes as hard as I could. The car swerved to the side and ended up on the shoulder of the highway. Catching my breath, I realized that I had fallen asleep at the wheel! A few more seconds and I would have crashed into a steel pole.

I got out of the car and walked around it to check for any fresh dents or scratches. Then I looked at the sky, now covered in sparse clouds, and at the pale moon, fading in the rays of dawn. I saw dark bird in the sky flying away. His weak screams— "Kee-eeeee-arr"—reached me. The bird was getting smaller and smaller till it eventually turned into a small dot and finally disappeared.

* * *

The next day I wanted to take my dad to a shrink to get him some psych pills. I even offered to stay at his place for a while. He declined it all. Instead, he said he has another plan and will follow it.

"Another plan? What's this?"

My dad tensed his face. "Woman. I need a woman," he said, overcoming his partial embarrassment.

"What do you mean, Dad? What are you talking about?"

"Fuck! I need a very good fuck! That's what I mean."

"Are you sure it will work?" I asked carefully, wrinkling my face. I still thought he was joking, or it was another delusion of his. Also, I was a little uncomfortable discussing this matter with him.

"Yes, I'm positive." My father now looked like a man who made the decision.

"How do you imagine this taking place?" I asked after a brief silence. "How would you find one? I'm sure all the strip clubs are closed. I heard that many working girls quit their jobs out of fear of COVID and stay home collecting unemployment."

"I'll figure it out. I'll look at some ads in the newspapers or on TV."

"They say the price for sex-services is now skyrocketing." I still tried to discourage him from pursuing his plan.

"Don't worry. I'll find someone who'll charge me decently," he replied.

I didn't believe anything good could come of this shenanigan and continued to argue with him. But I also knew that my father was weak when it came to women, and to be frank, despite not having robust health, he was very strong sexually. I remember how, in my childhood, I'd hear at night the conversations of my parents in the next bedroom, when my mother complained about his high sexuality, which was clearly a burden to her. Then his second wife unequivocally revealed the same thing in such a way that it was embarrassing for me to hear about it.

Maybe my dad is right. Could the problem be resolved in such a simple, natural way?

"Okay, Dad, do whatever you want."

The ball began to roll. After a few days, he called and asked me not to come over for a while. A week passed and finally he reappeared, telling me that everything was alright and that he was waiting for me because he missed me. When I went to see him, he was in good shape; he no longer complained and didn't tremble at the sight of his own shadow. Some self-satisfaction returned to him as well, even his former boorishness.

Sometime later, my dad informed me he had been at the cemetery recently and had bought a plot near my mother's grave.

"This issue should have been handled a long time ago, but I kept postponing it. When you visit your mother, maybe you'll also glance at me and read Kaddish over my grave."

Showdown

"**W**ho is it?" I asked, looking at the video screen of the intercom on the wall in my living room. Some Black man in a red baseball cap and wearing a black mask was standing in the lobby, facing the front door.

"FedEx delivery," he answered.

I brought my finger closer to the entrance button, but some force held me back from pressing it. Something about this man was vaguely familiar, as if we had already met, and clearly not for a prior FedEx delivery.

"Give me a second," I said, biting my lip, deciding what to do next.

"Hello, bro. What's up?" the man said when I finally opened the door of my apartment. He immediately stepped his foot over the threshold in case I tried to close the door.

"Hello," I replied, not moving, and looking directly at him.

The man was probably half a head taller than me. He was a bit thin, with an athletic build. Aside from the red baseball cap, he had on wide jeans and a white, untucked short-sleeved T-shirt with "BLM" written on it.

He took off his facemask and smiled broadly.

"What's up, bro? Do you recognize me? I'm Mr. Jason, Amy's boyfriend. How are things at the probation department? Are you still stalking ex-convicts? You played me well that time. That usually calls for a broken skull." He got quiet, glaring at me with a heavy, intense look.

From the hall outside came the sound of the elevator doors opening. Someone came out, and soon my neighbor's door slammed loudly around the corner.

"Bro, you don't even invite me into your house? It's not polite. I invited you to my place. Or since you're White, maybe you don't want to let a Black dude in? It's beneath you, huh?" He began to look over my head.

"How did you find out where I live?"

"How? Very simple. I called the probation department and gave them your name. I told them that my name was Jason and who I was. I told them that while I was in prison, you were fucking my shorty. And they immediately gave me your address. I came here to thank you for that." All this time he tried to look inside my apartment, probably expecting to see, if not Amy herself, then some traces of her being there. "Okay, man. Let's talk. I don't like beating around the bush. I like straight talk." Without waiting for an invitation, he pushed me away with a sharp thrust and entered the apartment.

Wheezing, I stood by the closet, crossing my arms on my chest.

Jason stood in the center of the living room, looking around. Without saying a word, then he checked the bedroom then looked into the bathroom.

"You don't have to search. She's not here."

My guest stopped a few steps across from me.

"Where is she? You should know."

"I wish I did, but I don't. She left more than a month ago; she disappeared. I don't know where she went or where she is now. She took ten thousand bucks 'for the road' from my dad, by the way," I said lying. "I thought *you* knew where she is."

Jason narrowed his eyes a little, his gaze remaining just as alert and suspicious. It was as if he was weighing whether my words were credible.

"She got ten grand from your dad? She's back to her old ways," he said, chuckling. It seemed he felt better that Amy's disappearance wasn't just unpleasant for him alone.

But the smile quickly left his face as his nostrils began to flare and the nodules twitched on his wide cheekbones.

"Yo, if you're bullshitting me again, you'll regret it." He extended his index finger, as if imitating the muzzle of a gun, and pointed it at me. "Pow! Pow! Just like that. Got it?"

I was silent.

"Answer! Do you get it?"

I nodded silently, but it wasn't a sign of acquiescence but rather that I heard him and understood—not necessarily that I was going to do what he wants.

"She sometimes remembered you. She was waiting for you to get out of prison. I offered her to live with me, but she refused. Apparently, she didn't want to stay with you, either. She chose neither of us. She picked herself instead. That's all I can tell you."

In a split second, Jason was in my face, grabbing me by the T-shirt.

"Don't tell me this shit! Don't tell me! Do you hear me? She didn't leave me, because she would never leave me! She knows what she is to me and that I would do anything for her. I can break you in half now if I want to, but I won't because she…" He stopped, as if not knowing how to end the sentence. Unclenching his fists from my T-shirt, he pushed me away. "Live, nigga. And stay the hell away from her. You better stay away."

He headed to the front door to leave, noticing Amy's slippers among my shoes and a few bottles of nail polish on the shelf. He shot me a disgusted look, but it seemed clear to him that the owner of these accessories no longer lived in this apartment.

"Do you want a drink?" I asked, just as he reached the door.

Jason froze at the unexpected offer. He slowly turned and, tilting his head to one side, looked at me as if seeing me for the first time.

"What? You're offering me a drink?"

"Why not?"

Without waiting for a response, I went to the dresser and took out an opened bottle of Absolut vodka and a full bottle of Johnny Walker Black Label. I placed two large shot glasses and two cups of water on the table, opened a jar of olives, and pulled out Pepsi, seltzer, apples, and cheese from the fridge.

Jason watched this scene unfold, not knowing how to react.

"Vodka? Whisky? What'll you have?" I asked him, pouring a glass of whisky for myself.

"Whisky, please," he said as he finally walked over to the table. He sat on a chair and removed the red baseball cap from his head.

The first three glasses we drank in silence — in absolute silence. When we drank the fourth, we began to drop some random phrases about the weather.

"Alexa, play 'Whisky Bar,'" I commanded.

"'Alabama Song' by The Doors," Alexa responded, and music began to play in the apartment.

"Alexa, stop it! Play Pop Smoke, 'Welcome to the Party,'" Jason interrupted, and Alexa obeyed, switching to rap.

"Fucking pandemic, the Chinese are trying to kill us Americans," Jason said, knocking back another shot of whisky. Then he took an apple, rubbed it on his T-shirt, and with a loud crunch, bit into it, splattering its juice.

"Yeah, the whole situation is fucking crazy," I agreed, drinking another glass myself.

"Fucking Trump," Jason said. "He should go to jail. The brothers at Rikers are waiting for him. He didn't even pay taxes, that motherfucker."

"Yeah, fuck him."

We poured more liquor into our glasses and drank after clinking them together.

"What are you going to do now?" I asked.

"I don't know. I wanted to get a job as a trainer in the fitness club where I used to work, but it's closed because of COVID. I'll have to look for something else. My PO is on my ass and wants me to get a job." He got quiet. "For the two years I was in prison, day and night I dreamed about the day I would get out, how I would start living together with her and everything would be okay. We would have a family and children. Yes, I assumed she would fuck someone else; I understand she's a woman and she has needs, but I was sure that when I came back, she would leave all her fuck boys and be with me. Ah! What a girl! One in a million."

"Yes, she is."

We had already emptied the bottle of whisky and started on the vodka. We were both really drunk. But we continued to drink, talking freely more than listening. Our conversation thus far had made little sense, but it was gaining significance and meaning.

"Yo, just imagine what's going on in jail right now because of this COVID. All the guys are sick; there are no masks, no treatment, nothing—just fucking nothing." He waved his hand, almost knocking over a glass on the table. "But for me, COVID brought luck. I was released three months early. And three months in prison, bro, that's a very long time, especially if it's the last three months. It's a verrrry long time. Have you ever done time? Well, yeah, not you. It's us Blacks— we get thrown in prison for any nonsense, and you Whites commit serious crimes, and you get away with everything."

"Can't disagree—racism hasn't gone anywhere. I always noticed the hidden side eyes and judgment we got from everyone when we were together. And when I was with a White woman, no one gave a shit at all."

"So, bro, you've experienced racism too," Jason joked. "Well, we Blacks face it at every turn. Do you know how my childhood started? It started on the playground outside our house. My dad took me there when I was about five years old and said, 'Son, remember, you're Black, but you're going to have to grow up among Whites who will always despise and hate you. So you have to be strong.' You know, it's not just I don't like you, and you me. It goes much deeper. This dates all the way to the times of slavery, when you Whites treated us worse than domestic animals."

"I just understand this very well. Because we Jews have experienced the same thing as you in our history."

"Maybe you're right. Although we Blacks suffered much more."

"Hey, hey, stop talking so much bullshit and playing the victim!" I exploded. "I understand everything, but let's talk directly about you. I know your story. You and Amy were selling drugs, then you got mixed up with criminals and started doing extortion. You deserved jail time."

"What? What are you talking about, man? What the fuck are you talking about? You, bro, are a fucking idiot and have no clue." Sweeping his arm widely, Jason knocked everything off the table in one motion. The plates, shot glasses, cans, and empty bottles flew to the floor.

"It's not me but you are being the idiot. You're the fucking idiot!" I enunciated clearly, moving forward and bringing my face closer to him. "She's not going to come back to you, anyway. She won't ever come back. Believe me. She'll come back to me. Remember what I'm telling you."

Now it became clear to both of us that this "peaceful gathering," with drinks and snacks, was only a warm-up—a prelude to the start of a completely different conversation.

I heard the loud bang of a strong slap, and my head jerked from the blow. I clenched my fists, but suddenly, instead of rushing at Jason, I laughed loudly and defiantly in his face.

"She doesn't need you, bro! You're nobody and nothing! I've seen a bunch of people like you. You won't last being clean. Mark my words. In a month you'll be a criminal again, and by the end of the year you'll be back in jail. Got it? And Amy will live with me. And she'll fuck me, and she'll love me, and she'll give me blowjobs…" I didn't have time to finish my tirade when Jason clenched his fist and slammed it into my chest.

"Fuuuck!" I yelled, dropping to the floor. But I quickly jumped to my feet and, leaning to the side, tried to punch Jason, who by that time was already standing in front of me in a boxing stance.

Defending himself from my blow, he punched me hard in the stomach and then hit me in the jaw from below with an uppercut.

My eyes darkened. Though very drunk, I felt a salty taste in my mouth as blood spilled out from my nose. Breathing heavily, watching the blood begin to drip from my nose onto my white T-shirt, I put my right hand behind my back and—moments later—I held a gun in my hand pointed at Jason.

"Get out of my house! Do you hear me?"

Jason stopped, shocked at the turn of events, and instinctively leaned backward. He stared at the gun in my hand.

"Out! Fucking out of my house!" I gasped.

I now clearly realized the main reason for me getting the gun—confronting Jason, because I knew that sooner or later, we would run into each other.

I was overcome with real madness. Despite this, I was still aware that under no circumstances would I remove the pistol from its safety.

Suddenly, something dark flashed before my eyes. It was Jason's hand, and in a split second I flew into a corner of the floor.

Getting on top of me, Jason attempted to pry the gun I still managed to hold. He clung to it unclenching my fingers, but I slammed his ribs with my free hand and then dug it into his face, trying to pierce his eyes with my fingers. He tried to rip my hand away, but I hit him in the chest with the butt of the gun and escaped his grasp.

I stood up again. Everything was a blur. Blood was pouring from my nose, and my T-shirt, hands, and jeans were all covered in it.

To my surprise, Jason stood up quietly, cracked his joints, straightened his back, and put his hand to his chest, as if checking himself for signs of injury. Then, tilting his head to one side and raising his right eyebrow in surprise, he looked at me, just as he had looked at me shortly before this, when I offered him a drink.

"You, bro, are a real fighter. Now I understand why Amy got together with you. Listen, I have nothing against you, bro. We got to know each other today, right? But for now, you and I better not meet. Because it could end badly for one of us, probably for both of us. I can't promise you anything."

"Me too."

Jason's face flinched, but he quickly got a hold of himself and grinned again. "I understand—you don't know how to keep your fucking mouth shut. It's a very bad trait, bro. Okay, enough for today. It's time for me to go." He cracked his fingers demonstratively, walked over to the table, and picked up the red baseball cap lying there. "Here's another thing: I advise you to get rid of this toy. Bro, you can't kill anyone; I can see you're not the kind of person who can kill. And five years in prison for illegal possession of a weapon is guaranteed. Or maybe you'll keep this gun just for me now?"

"Thanks for your advice, but I own it legally," I said, wiping the blood off my chin.

PART SIX

Turd in the Punchbowl

I t was a lovely Sunday afternoon; the summer sun was enveloping New York in its gentle light. Birds were chirping everywhere. The air was filled with the aroma of herbs and flowers.

My ER shift fell on this day. Even though the shift fell on a Sunday, most of the employees in the ER were in high spirits. Maybe it was because summer was in full swing.

Or it could have been because there were very few patients in the ER that morning—almost a third of the units were empty. Although all the workers followed the strict superstition not to utter the "Q" word, each of us was aware that, indeed, it was really quiet.

But the main reason for the general mood elevation was definitely because truck arrived and took away the three mobile mortuaries that morning. Their space was now free, and the last reminder of that ominous symbol of the pandemic was the drying asphalt where water from their refrigeration units had dripped.

On this day our staff allowed themselves to relax a little. Some looked at websites on computers, while others read the news and still others chatted amongst themselves. Some propped up their foreheads with their hands and just dozed off.

I was talking with giant technician Steven, occasionally glancing at the clock. When there is no work and nothing to do, time drags on.

In the dimwit zone, only one middle-aged man, in a yellow gown, was lying quietly and peacefully on a bed, snoozing.

"The guy is a war vet," Steven informed me. "He put on a show last night at the veterans' home he lives: he got into a fight with the tenants and threatened to blow up the building. He's already been seen by a psychiatrist and ordered to the cuckoo house. We're waiting for his bed to be prepared there."

"I see."

We both took another look at the man and, not noticing anything particular about him, shifted the conversation to something else. After chatting with Steven, I went to my office.

"Ben! Ben! Are you there?" Dr. Harris called me from his office. He was also working that day.

"Yes, doc."

"Come here, man."

Soon I was standing at the entrance to his office.

"Ben, how is your girlfriend doing? HR is still working on her case, and they say they need one more signature to get her on board. It takes no more than few weeks."

I was silent.

"Ben, did you hear what I just said or are you deaf?"

"Truth be told, I don't know where Amy is right now, what is going on with her, or if she'll be back at all," I confessed with a sigh.

"Oh, so that's it. What a pity. I liked her, good girl." It was evident that Dr. Harris felt some pity. "By the way, are the recent bruises on your face somehow related to her disappearance?"

"You could say that. I accidentally bumped into her ex-boyfriend, and we had a tough talk over a bottle of vodka."

"Don't despair buddy. Maybe she'll come back." He didn't know what else to say to me in consolation. But it was clear that he had invited me over for some other reason. "Ben, look I know that you have a Shakespearean tragedy on your hands and don't much care about anything else, but I really need your help with something. Then listen carefully. You know the refrigerator in the corner of the conference room? There are twenty packs of hot dogs in there that I bought, and a large pot of sauerkraut. In the lockers you'll find napkins and disposable utensils. Ask the residents to help you. Take a medicine cart, load everything on it, and take it outside. I'll meet you there."

Soon several of us were standing near the ER on a small, green lawn. Dr. Harris pulled a grill out of the trunk of his car and plugged a gas cylinder into it. Together with two residents, we set up folding tables and began to grill the hot dogs.

The residents found a speaker and were playing music. They talked among themselves, arguing about hemoglobin and potassium in the blood while they turned the hot dogs over on the grill. Soon, fragrant steam was rising over the thin rows of cooked hot dogs lying on foil. It also smelled of sauerkraut, which Dr. Harris was distributing in gray plastic tubs in which nurses normally carried bandages, medicines, and syringes for injections.

Then, from the building to the "restaurant," the first "customers" started arriving. Nurses, cops, and maintenance workers exited the sliding doors.

I offered them options: "Chicken, beef, or pork?"

"Mmmm, yummy. Ben, give me one more."

Occasionally, after turning off the main highway, EMTs drove past us, bringing in new patients.

"Hey guys! Want a hot dog?" I shouted to the paramedics waving raised empty plates.

"Yes!!" they yelled, stopping their cars.

I passed a paper plate with hotdogs to one of my colleagues standing nearby, and he would bring it to the EMTs.

During this time, while I was distributing the hot dogs, I didn't even notice the strange commotion taking place nearby. A policeman dropped his hot dog and ran off; the head nurse and Dr. Harris took off after him.

"Escaped! Escaped!" We heard shouts, and many of the staff rushed in the direction of a narrow one-way road outside the grounds of the hospital.

I also left the restaurant and hurried to where a group of people had gathered near the road.

"I'm a veteran. Yes! A veteran of the war in Afghanistan! Fuck all of you guys!" A thickset middle-aged man in a yellow hospital gown and with only socks on his feet stood surrounded by our workers. "Get out of my way!" he shouted.

"I see that you're a veteran. But you have to calm down. Do you hear me?" Dr. Harris stood opposite the raging man, addressing him in a soothing but firm voice. "Listen to me. You have to go back to the ER right now. Do you hear me?"

"Fuck off, asshole!" Stepping forward, the man raised his fist to punch Dr. Harris in the face.

Just then, a policeman standing nearby grabbed him by the arm and, after a short struggle, wrestled him to the ground. The man was still trying to escape. I jumped in dropping to the ground, I put my whole body on the man's legs so he couldn't get up.

"Stretcher! Get a stretcher here!" Dr. Harris ordered and, without waiting, he ran to the hospital building for a bed.

A few more cops came to the "place of battle."

"Who is he?" "What happened to him?" "How did he manage to escape?" the coworkers were asking one another.

A nurse explained: "He was lying in the ER, waiting for a free bed in the cuckoo house. He seemed to be fine. Then he got up to supposedly go to the toilet. But in fact, he snuck to the back of the corridor, where the locked emergency exit glass door is. He broke the glass with a fire extinguisher and ran out. But the siren turned on, and he didn't get far."

The gathered staff commented on the event: "It's nothing surprising. He is a war veteran; he must have imagined that he was captured by the terrorists." "These veterans are unhappy folk; their brains are totally screwed up because of the war."

In the meantime, a stretcher was brought to the scene.

"We're putting you down and taking you back to the ER," Dr. Harris said as he knelt down on one knee in front of the subdued man, who was lying on the ground in his yellow gown as we held him tightly by the arms and legs. Dr. Harris was clutching black leather straps. "Listen to me, my friend. If you promise to behave normally, we won't strap you to the side rails. Choose: yes or no?"

"Yes," the man answered in a flat voice.

"Okay. But mind me, no funny business. Let's go." Dr. Harris signaled with his hand, and we lifted the man from the ground.

He reluctantly lay down on the stretcher.

The policemen raised the side rails. "Ready? Let's go." We rolled the stretcher toward the hospital.

"Once I get out of this hospital, I'll get an M-16, come back here, and make rock 'n roll for all of you," the patient said while casting us dirty looks. "Or I'll find out where you guys live and come and kill each of you!"

"Man, can you shut up?!" Dr. Harris said commandingly.

Surprisingly, the man obeyed and shut up.

Pushing the bed as we walked, Dr. Harris looked at me and said, "I was lulled into a sense of security and thought at least today would be quiet. Like hell!"

We were passing the "restaurant". The police officers and Dr. Harris pushed the stretcher further toward the entrance of the ER. I stayed outside to continue serving our coworkers and EMS personnel.

It was loud and joyful. "Chicken or beef?" "Ketchup or mustard?" "Mmmm, yummy. Give me one more." We were joking, laughing, and taking pictures for memory. We all knew the pandemic wasn't over — scientists warned about a second wave in late fall, and of new and more dangerous virus variants. We didn't want to think about it that day. We withstood the first blow; that was enough for now.

It was a real hot dog bonanza — with the most delicious hot dogs I'd ever eaten in my life.

A Distant Voice

Out of the blue one day, Amy called me. Instead of the phone number, the Caller ID on my mobile phone flashed "Private Number."

"Ben, hi."

"Hi."

"How's it going?"

"Fine. And you?"

"Me too. You know, when I was leaving, I was in such a rush that I forgot to give you back the keys to your apartment. Every time I wanted to send them back to you, it just didn't work out."

"It's not a problem. Do as you please. How is your novel going?"

"My novel? You know, it turned out that writing a novel is a hard job, much harder than I expected. It's 24/7. Some characters and chapters are coming out great while others are very primitive, real garbage. When something isn't working out, I'm anguished, literally on a physical level. I fall into despair, feel hatred for everyone and everything. Just when I'm ready to give up, tear up all the drafts, and delete all the digital versions, suddenly a unique literary thought occurs to me. That's when I experience real bliss. Overall, I'll be finished with it very soon. It will be my first novel."

"I'm glad."

"By the way, I have good news. My probation is over. I'm gonna get my nursing license restored soon and I'll be able to work as a nurse. So, everything in my life is coming together. God is good." She kept silent again.

It was so silent that I could hear her breathing on the other end of the line. It dawned on me that now Amy wanted to say something very important, which was the reason she called in the first place. My heart started beating rapidly.

"Ben, you know, I finally figured things out and understood who it is I really need. I know for sure now who I love and what man loves me… I wanted to ask if you were seeing anyone?"

"Hmm. Am I seeing someone? Yes, a nurse from our department who was hired recently. She's young and beautiful. We started dating about a month ago."

"You're not joking?" she asked cautiously.

"No, I'm serious. All the jokes are over," I replied, feeling my heart would explode with happiness.

There was a short pause. I expected Amy to become enraged, throwing accusations and insults. Then I would confess that I was playing a joke on her and just couldn't live without her. I was blessed that she finally made her decision and chose me!

"How dare you," she quietly said. "You threw me to hell. To hell."

The line went dead.

I waited until night and could barely sleep, leaving my cell on the pillow next to me and turning up the volume to the max so, God forbid, I wouldn't miss her call. Amy never called back.

After a few days, I received a package with the keys from her. I decided that it didn't mean anything and continued waiting. Now I often left my door unlocked in case Amy decided to return by surprise and I wouldn't be home.

"I'm such a unique idiot!" I repeated this phrase every day from morning to night.

Like Father, Like Son

I saw my father much more often than before. Now he came to me more than I to him. He was not in need of anyone's care anymore.

He got a job as a volunteer in a Jewish charity organization, helping to pack food in boxes, and for this he received "tips" in the form of additional produce and other foodstuffs on top of his usual food ration. I'd given him a set of keys to my apartment, so every other week he'd either bring or leave me bags of canned salmon, chocolate, cans of coffee, cheese, meat, vegetables, and fruits—all of exceptional quality. I really didn't need any of this food at all, but played along because it kept my father busy, and he felt needed. It was also obvious that I couldn't eat it all myself, but I didn't want to offend him, so I accepted everything he brought, thanked him, and then gave away most of it to my neighbors.

More importantly, there were changes in our relationship beyond the domestic and superficial—deep changes I think we both felt. We began to talk more often heart to heart, and we argued and quarreled less often.

At the dinner table, he began to cautiously start conversations about whether I wanted to change something in my personal life. Namely, would I want to return to my ex-wife and daughter? He even offered to be the mediator. This was just old age talking, and the desire to surround himself with dear people—a kind of warm family circle—as he came closer to the cold end.

I made it clear to him that ship had sailed, and that Sarah, Veronica, and I had lived separate lives for many years now and there was no going back. "We never even much inquired about each other. Sarah had a boyfriend with whom she had been living for a few years; maybe she'd even married him. I didn't know for sure, nor did I want to. It's true, I don't ask about Veronica much. The only thing I do for her is pay child support and send her money for her birthday and Hanukkah. I know—I'm a pathetic excuse for a father, and wasn't much of a husband either, but we're not uncommon, right Dad?" He knew what I was implying.

Sometimes he inquired about Amy. "Where is she? Do you hear anything from her?" In conversations with me, he didn't refer to her with derogatory names, but never referred to her by her real name either.

"Dad c'mon—what she's up to, where she is, when she'll come back, and even if she'll come back at all, I really don't know."

Hearing this, my father would nod silently. His facial expression revealed that he was very satisfied with this answer.

"Don't worry about her, son. I guarantee you she's got a new fucker to drag money out of. She already forgot about you, so why don't you forget about her."

His distaste for Amy caused me deep frustration. Yes, it sucked. But it didn't matter that much anyway since she was not with me anymore.

I asked my father about his heart surgeries and his symptoms before and after each one. I meticulously questioned him about what kind of pain he had, stabbing or dull. Answering my questions, he talked repeatedly about that ill-fated day when he fell on the street on the way to his car and when "his heart seemed to be torn in half." After that, once in the hospital, they discovered a whole bunch of heart issues he had not even suspected.

"Why do you need to know all this?" He asked me. "The main thing is they fixed me; the pacemaker and stents are in place, and the pills help. God willing, I'll live for some time."

"I'm interested purely from a medical point of view," I replied. "After all, I work in the ER and need as much medical knowledge as I can get."

Several times we went together to the beach—to Plumb Beach and Far Rockaway—where we sat on the sandy shore in sun loungers, watching the sailboats and surfers, and enjoying the sunsets. Our bodies were covered with beautiful bronze tans.

My father's features still maintained their elasticity and energy, but in his posture, an old man's stoop had appeared. His muscles were noticeably losing their firmness, and his gait had less surety.

Nevertheless, looking at him, I now recognized him in myself more and more—and myself in him—experiencing a strange feeling of duality, or rather, a kind of oneness with my father. Amy would say more than once, "Ben, you're a copy of your father—just a clone, both on the inside and outside. It's genetics. Like him, you're superficially social, but deep inside, you're a very lonely man." I tried not to attach much importance to her words. I never wanted to resemble him, either externally or internally. I've always considered myself to be his exact opposite.

Now, smoothing my hair, stretching, shaving in front of the mirror, in facial expressions, gestures, and tastes—even choosing a new watch with a specific wristband—I often caught myself thinking that I inherited a lot from my father. Even my habit of making silly jokes—whether appropriate or out of place, which could potentially have serious, even fatal consequences—I definitely picked up from him. I'm the flesh of his flesh, the spirit of his spirit, whether I like it or not. My character also resembles his, and our destinies are also similar in multiple ways.

Eventually, I noticed that he was deteriorating, not just physically, but also mentally. He began to forget people's names and street names, and he became suspicious of things. His driving skills worsened, most likely because he was too tense behind the wheel since he couldn't depend on his memory and quick reaction. He admitted to me that a couple of times he couldn't remember where he had put money, which would never have happened to him before under any circumstances. His judgment was also not as deep and true as before.

But strangely, the more I noticed all these weaknesses in him, the closer I felt to him. Like some inner magnets were drawing us closer to each other. All of the shortcomings that I once found intolerable and which caused in me persistent hostility and irritation—his bad character, rudeness, callousness, proclivity to scandal—I now perceived and accepted with total calm. I even wondered why these traits of his incensed and distressed me to such an extent before. Why did I constantly wait for and demand something from him? Yes, I wanted him to be different. But he wasn't supposed to be different. He was given to me like this. Fate had chosen him specifically to be my father. Him, not someone else.

Nothing became an obstacle in our newly arisen love for each other—except I heard the ticking of the clock very clearly. I parted with what I thought was a harmless illusion: that everything in life can be changed and corrected—it's never too late. That was a very dangerous line of thinking. Instead, I clearly understood that life is like a river, flowing in only one direction and never in reverse. Every day, the course of life takes away a piece of us, taking us somewhere into the unknown, from where no one will ever return.

I remember my mother, when we spoke about my father, always repeated the same thing: "Forgive him. You have to learn to forgive, my son." My mom knew how to forgive. I tried to learn this art from her—the art of forgiveness. And I succeeded in many ways. I forgave my colleagues at work, my relatives, and my friends for their slight and even significant trespasses. I knew I wasn't without sin either and was counting on forgiveness from others too. I knew that resentment and hatred undermine and destroy from within, while forgiveness heals. I learned to forgive everyone except for him, no matter how hard I tried to do it.

And so, when I no longer hoped that this would ever happen, I suddenly found some profound changes in my soul. They began to happen on their own, against my will and almost without any effort. I was rediscovering my father—this man I had always known but never accepted or loved—in new ways. Who knows, maybe I loved him after all, but it was very difficult for me to get to that love and find the core of its existence.

It was only then, during the dangerous pandemic and when he began to noticeably deteriorate, that I learned what forgiveness and love for my father really was.

One day, my dad informed me that he had drawn up a power of attorney that gave me the right to control and use all his savings, which he'd stored in his bank accounts. Three hundred and fifty thousand dollars! "I have almost nothing to spend this money on — how much do I need to exist? I have no one to give it to but you."

Such a surprising gesture! Actually, I expected this to happen.

Listen to Your Heart

One day I was wandering around the salt marsh. Stopping, I looked for a long time at the towering falcon's nest in the distance. There was nothing in it; over the summer, the chicks had grown and flown away. On one of the pillars not far from the nest, a falcon sat: a motionless dark spot, its wings folded.

I looked at it, and episodes flashed through my memory from when Amy first saw these birds here and immediately believed that the soul of a falcon had entered into her. And how bizarrely after that the falcon "theme" was woven into our lives, giving both of us wonderful, unforgettable minutes.

Now the falcon sitting on the pole looked ugly. I decided that I should shoot this bird. Only in this way would I gain freedom and finally be rid of the bird obsession and Amy's memory along with it.

"Enough. This can't go on for much longer! The reality is that she dumped me and left. God only knows what she's up to. Maybe my dad was right: she got a new boyfriend to suck money out of. She's not reliable, like a migratory bird that you know will be returning. I have to forget her, take care of myself, and find a woman to date. But first, I must kill the bird."

When I got home, I opened the metal box where I stored the Glock and ammo. I loaded the magazine into the gun and cocked it. Then I pointed the gun at the empty window. The gun wasn't heavy, and the handle was very comfortable.

"*Finita la commedia.*"

I was about to leave the apartment to go to the salt marsh, but after a few steps I suddenly felt shooting pains in my heart again. In recent months, I'd felt it tingling throughout the day to varying degrees. (That's why I so meticulously questioned my father about his heart issues.) But in the last week, I'd wake up at night from a sudden, strong heartbeat, and for a long time couldn't fall back asleep till it calmed down. Then in the next days, I'd be overcome with severe weakness. And now, at this moment, I felt it become very cold in my chest, and it was hard for me to breathe. A huge glacial abyss seemed to occupy where my heart had been. I took another step and stuck my hand out against the closet door to hold myself, panting. I stood, leaning over, and afraid to move.

"Ah!"

My legs buckled, and I collapsed to the floor. I lay there, unable to move my arms or legs. I was cold all over, but it felt freezing in my chest. I don't know exactly how long I was lying there. I didn't even know if I was lying on my side or on my back. I faintly heard the intercom bell ring. But I didn't care; I wasn't expecting anything, and I wasn't hoping for anything. I felt something like a sharp beak begin to rip into and tear apart my chest.

"Sorry baby, I was wrong, I shouldn't have even considered doing it," I said in my head.

I just waited patiently for the last thread to break.

"Oh, Ben! Sonny…my boy…what's happened?!" I heard my father's voice overhead. It sounded somehow low and vague, as if it were coming from somewhere far, far away— thousands of miles away. "Benny, where does it hurt? You're not drunk, no? What's wrong with you! Is this a…What the fuck is this, a gun?! Are you alive? Wounded?" He started grabbing me all over. "Son, did you want to kill yourself?!"

Then I vaguely heard my father shouting something on the phone, calling out my first and last names and the address of my house. "Yes, now!! Forty years old. I'm his father. He's lying down and can't get up. He can't talk. Yes, he's breathing. Please get here now!!"

He was kneeling in front of me. I think he was crying. I felt him put a pillow under my head, and then he lifted my T-shirt and began to stroke my chest. "Benny, Benny. Could that be your heart? Did I really give you my damn heart disease as well? Be quiet, be quiet, son. They'll be here soon. They're coming now. And I brought you a package of groceries. It's a good ration with canned food, cheese, fruits, and chocolate candy—the kind you like. I was calling the apartment, but you didn't answer. So, I decided to bring it in, and here you are on the floor! And there's a gun on the floor! You dummy, what are you doing with your life…"

* * *

I was lying on a bed in the ER of my hospital, an IV stretching from my arm and a medicine bag hanging over my head on a metal hook.

"Have you had chest pains for a long time?" asked Dr. Harris, who was standing in front of me.

"Yes, these last months. At first, I barely noticed them. But then the pain intensified, and in the last week it began to hurt so much that I couldn't sleep. I was going to go to a cardiologist, but I kept finding excuses not to do it. I thought it would somehow resolve on its own."

"We ran several tests and are waiting for the results," Dr. Harris looked at the electronic sensors beeping behind my head. "One thing I can tell you for sure, buddy, you have COVID. We just got the test result. Apparently from prolonged stress, you first started to have some heart problems, and then COVID made everything worse. Your love story also screwed you over."

In a minute, Dr. Mercy walked over with his determined walk of a former marine, fixed his glasses and looked at the monitors as well. Both doctors looked at each other and briefly exchanged words using medical terms that I didn't know.

"Boy, mark my word, you'll get rest and live up to a hundred years," he said firmly. "You know, your dad is in the waiting area asking permission to see you, but I don't think it's a good idea right now. I'll go talk to him and reassure him that everything is under control."

"Cool." I closed my eyes. It became easier for me — easier to breathe, easier to think, easier to speak.

The End of the Novel

I took sick leave and rested for a month. I relaxed, read a lot, and listened to music. I thought about my distant past, present, and everything that had recently been happening.

One time I asked my dad what had happened to the gun. I guessed that he had taken it.

"I sold it for a million dollars," he answered me with deep anger.

After that, we didn't discuss it anymore.

* * *

I spent a lot of time in the salt marsh in autumn, wandering along the coast and along its winding paths. I watched the amazing, bustling, and eventful life of the various creatures. The smells of salt water, damp earth, and wet rocks penetrated my nostrils. I felt inextricably merged with this world that had existed billions of years before me—a tiny particle—and which would go on well after my departure…

One day, I was sitting on the shore with my fishing pole. Suddenly, I heard, "Kee-eeeee-arr!" The familiar, anxious, and joyful scream was coming not from the sky but the ground. Rising—obeying some incomprehensible force— I dropped the rod and rushed into a grove where the cries seemed to be coming from, jumping over fallen branches and ravines, tripping and falling over exposed tree roots, and scaring stray cats and raccoons.

"Kee-eeeee-arr!" The bird kept screaming. Its cries surrounded me, creating the illusion it was close to me and far away at the same time.

Finally, I understood where they were coming from and where the falcon was. In a torn T-shirt and covered in marsh debris, I left the salt marsh and hurried home. I was sure that Amy had returned!

To my surprise, Jason, her boyfriend, was standing in front of the building.

"Hey, bro," he said, blocking my way.

"Hello." I tensed all over, preparing for another "heavy male conversation." But Jason didn't seem to be in a fighting mood at all; on the contrary, he was somehow depressed, unhappy.

"Relax, bro. I didn't come for that. I came to tell you not to wait for her anymore. She won't be coming back to you. She…" He trailed off, wrinkling his forehead so hard. "She died."

"What nonsense are you telling me?! You're lying!"

"I got a call from her stepfather. We met when Amy and I went to Georgia to visit her relatives a few years ago."

"How did it happen?" I couldn't believe what I just heard.

"Seizure. It happened when she recently returned to Georgia and was looking for work. You know her story with booze, right? You know how dangerous it was for her. She was aware of it very well… Bro, you were also involved in this tragedy. If you weren't in the picture, she would still be with me and alive. Alive!" He scrunched up his face, looking at me intently, and tears glistened in his eyes. "Your apartment's door is unlocked. Sorry, I came in without an invite. I left something there for you, you'll be surprised. So long," he tapped me lightly on the shoulder with his fist and left.

I entered my apartment. There in the living room was a book lying on the table: *Scream of the Falcon*, by Amy O'Neil. I picked up the book and skimmed through a few pages.

If I had a gun, that evening I would have put a bullet in my head.

* * *

Sometime later I sold my co-op and moved to another apartment on the other side of the city, away from Marine Park and the salt marsh, where everything reminded me of... her.

About the Author

PETR NEMIROVSKIY is a Ukrainian-American born in 1963 in Kiev, Ukraine. He graduated from Kiev University with a degree in journalism and started his career as a journalist and writer in 1997.

Nemirovskiy immigrated to the United States in 2000. He went on to get a master's in clinical social work in the US and has enjoyed a successful career in psychotherapy since then. On top of that, he's a professor at Fordham University, where he teaches substance abuse classes to graduate students.

Throughout this period, Nemirovskiy has continued to nurture his passion for writing. He's also worked as a psychotherapist, which has given him a deeper insight into human behavior and relationships. This has influenced and enriched his literary work. Seven of his books have been published in Ukraine and Russia. Nemirovskiy published his first novel, *A Walk Down Misery Street*, in 2022 to reach American readers.

From the beginning of the pandemic through its decline, Petr Nemirovskiy worked in the emergency department at a hospital in New York City. He transformed this experience into his new novel, *Scream of the Falcon*.

www.ingramcontent.com/pod-product-compliance
Lightning Source LLC
Chambersburg PA
CBHW060619310726
48982CB00003B/611